The Adventure of the Naked Guide

Conversation Pieces

A Small Paperback Series from Aqueduct Press
Subscriptions available: www.aqueductpress.com

About the Aqueduct Press
Conversation Pieces Series

The feminist engaged with sf is passionately interested in challenging the way things are, passionately determined to understand how everything works. It is my constant sense of our feminist-sf present as a grand conversation that enables me to trace its existence into the past and from there see its trajectory extending into our future. A genealogy for feminist sf would not constitute a chart depicting direct lineages but would offer us an ever-shifting, fluid mosaic, the individual tiles of which we will probably only ever partially access. What could be more in the spirit of feminist sf than to conceptualize a genealogy that explicitly manifests our own communities across not only space but also time?

Aqueduct's small paperback series, Conversation Pieces, aims to both document and facilitate the "grand conversation." The Conversation Pieces series presents a wide variety of texts, including short fiction (which may not always be sf and may not necessarily even be feminist), essays, speeches, manifestoes, poetry, interviews, correspondence, and group discussions. Many of the texts are reprinted material, but some are new. The grand conversation reaches at least as far back as Mary Shelley and extends, in our speculations and visions, into the continually created future. In Jonathan Goldberg's words, "To look forward to the history that will be, one must look at and retell the history that has been told." And that is what Conversation Pieces is all about.

L. Timmel Duchamp

Jonathan Goldberg, "The History That Will Be" in Louise
Fradenburg and Carla Freccero, eds., *Premodern Sexualities* (New
York and London: Routledge, 1996)

Praise for the Blood-Thirsty Agent series

The Adventure of the Incognita Countess

2017 Recommended Reading Lists of *Locus* and *Tangent Online*; *Seattle Times* list of noteworthy books of 2017.

"[A] brisk novella...it draws deeply from the well of 19th and early 20th century speculative literature. In that much, it reminds me no small part of Penny Dreadful. It has the same gleeful delight in its own references, the same playfully gothic geekery."
  —Liz Bourke, *Tor.com*

"[G]rand and smashing recursive steampunk…a splendid romp indeed."
  —Paul Di Filippo, *Asimov's*

The Adventure of the Dux Bellorum

"[A] gleeful mashup of historical and fictional characters... all good fun, not without more serious rumination on issues like colonialism and women's suffrage."
  —Rich Horton, *Locus*, April 2019

"This tale of two monsters, at once romantic and action-packed, is fun and thought-provoking, giving readers everything they want."
  —*Publisher's Weekly* (starred review)

"[T]he book takes all the elements of the first installment and builds on it. The action is more visceral, the cast larger, the stakes much higher. There are sapient dinosaurs, vampire vs. wolfman fights, and a particularly evil German scientist who just won't seem to die. Plus there are moments where the characters must confront their missions and the legacies of their nations. It's a fast-paced, daring adventure that is all kinds of Extra…."
  —Charles Payseur, *Quick Sip Reviews*

Conversation Pieces
Volume 74

The Adventure of the Naked Guide

by
Cynthia Ward

Published by Aqueduct Press
PO Box 95787
Seattle, WA 98145-2787
www.aqueductpress.com

ISBN: 978-1-61976-179-7

Cover design: Joe Murphy
Cover credits:
Background (landscape): National Gallery of Art/NGA
Images, Frederic Edwin Church, El Rio de Luz (The River of
Light), 1877
https://www.nga.gov/collection/art-object-page.50299.html
Cave mouth: Scopio, Through rock ring to sea, Margarita
Samsonova, https://scop.io/products/through-rock-ring-to-
sea?variant=27885275217943
Pterodactyls courtesy Joe Murphy
Original Block Print of Mary Shelley by Justin Kempton:
www.writersmugs.com

Acknowledgments

For their assistance and support, I'd like to acknowledge my late mother and thank my father, my sister, my brother-in-law, Steven J. Bigwood, Jessica "Jessie Lou" Butterfield, L. Timmel Duchamp, Win Scott Eckert, C.C. Finlay, Kim Fletcher, Dr. Donald M. Frazee, Lucas Garrett, Arrate Hidalgo, Dr. Kyung H. Lee, Saabrina Mosher, S., Nisi Shawl, Joe Vincent, Kathryn Wilham, Amy Wolf, and especially Dr. James Ray Comer, Rebecca McFarland Kyle, and Joe Murphy.

All mistakes are mine.

For C.C. Finlay, without whom there would be
no series of adventures

"Are there not other alternatives than sending our armies to chew barbed wire in Flanders?"
  —Winston Churchill, in a letter to Prime Minister H. H. Asquith

"I believe that this War, on which I entered as a war of defence and liberation, has now become a war of aggression and conquest."
  —Siegfried Sassoon, Soldier's Declaration Against the War

"There are times, young fellah, when every one of us must make a stand for human right and justice, or you never feel clean again."
  —Arthur Conan Doyle, *The Lost World*

"If your dear heart is wounded, my wild heart bleeds with yours."
  —J. Sheridan Le Fanu, "Carmilla"

Royal Dungeon, Lustadt, Kingdom of Lutha, Balkan Peninsula, 24 December 1916

"You've picked a posh meeting spot," I tell M as I walk into the cell. "I can only hope my assignment proves as cushy."

The head of the Empire's Secret Intelligence Service isn't the only man in the reeking cell. The other is a stranger, but I recognise him. He's about thirty. His gaunt face and form and his grey-threaded hair and beard suggest he's much older. He's chained to the floor.

I turn to M. He's a portly, towering mortal, with pale grey eyes and receding grey hair. He wears a British Army officer's trench coat and a Sam Browne belt, with a Webley Mk VI service revolver in the holster.

I address him. "The Luthanians are in the streets, celebrating their liberation from Austria and praying for the return of their missing king. Why the hell haven't you freed him? For that matter, why the hell are you here, instead of Petrograd?"

"I've just arrived," M replies. "Miss Harker, your language is deplorable."

I indicate the mortal in chains. "This isn't?"

The prone man speaks, his voice cracked by long privation. "Mr Holmes wants me to agree to a treaty which makes the kingdom of Lutha a protectorate of Britain."

M says, "Bernard Custer is an American adventurer of unknown loyalties, who seized the throne of this flyspeck of a nation under questionable circumstances."

"Mr Custer is a war hero who fought for his ancestral homeland against the Austrian invaders," I say. "He's king of Lutha because he's cousin and sole heir of the late king."

"I'm sure the Luthanians filled your ears with many interesting stories while you worked under cover in Lustadt," M says. "Mr Custer's provenance remains to be confirmed."

I return my attention to the emaciated man. "You'd not have treated Rudolf Rassendyll in this fashion."

"The late hero of Ruritania was a British intelligence operative," M replies.

King Bernhard tries to rise and sinks back, confined by weakness and short chains. Taking my skirt in hand, I sink to my knees beside him. His clothes are filthy rags, and he shivers with cold and weakness. I wrap him in my wool overcoat and keep an arm about him. His shoulder-blades feel like knives.

M says, "What do you think you're doing?"

Pushing back the right sleeve of my jacket, I extend my fangs and slash open my wrist.

The king's eyes widen, but he raises a hand to guide my bleeding wound to his lips.

He realises what I am.

M's eyes have narrowed so they appear as colourless as acid in the electric light. "Get away from Custer."

I let M read my lips. "Give me the sack."

He makes no response.

I'm one of only two blood-drinkers in the service of the British Empire.

The other is my lover.

I tell the King of Lutha, "Your wife is safe."

He doesn't take his mouth from my wrist, but his eyes are eloquent.

M says, "Miss Harker."

I don't bother looking at my stepfather as I reply. "If we didn't know whether my mother was alive or dead, we'd want to."

The king ceases to shiver. Colour suffuses his complexion and muscle thickens on his bones. When he firms the set of his shoulders and raises his head from my wrist, his eyes are keen.

I look at his iron cuffs, wondering if I've lost too much blood to break them, and M says, "You've done enough."

Hiding my weakened state, I stand. "You haven't."

"We've provided the man with food and water, as you can see, and I've sent for clothing."

From the corridor come the sounds of a surprisingly familiar pair of footsteps.

I tell M, "King Bernhard doesn't merit the dungeon."

"The old king of Lutha collaborated with the Austrians," M says. "Perhaps the new king did, as well."

King Bernhard speaks levelly, his voice strong. "That's absurd, and you know it."

I meet M's gaze. "Investigating someone's past doesn't justify his mistreatment."

"Defending the Empire justifies everything."

Noticing the footsteps, he turns his head, then gives me a look.

"Step out of the cell, Miss Harker."

Stiff with arthritis, he follows me into the corridor, which is lined with otherwise empty cells. Their smells are muted from disuse, and the ghosts of the dungeon have antique fashions. The Austrian invaders were keeping their royal captive isolated.

M and I face the living man who strides vigorously up the corridor. Tall and lean and young, he's dashing in the uniform of the Royal Tripod Corps. When his nostrils flare, I know he's scented the prisoner.

Though M is a civilian, my half-brother salutes him.

Then he looks at me with a sardonic lift of the eyebrows. "A curious place to observe your birthday, Lucy."

I smile grimly. "Woman proposes, M disposes."

Lieutenant Quincey Morris Holmes served originally as an aëroplane pilot on the Western Front. He re-trained for the Martian-style fighting-machines when Prime Minister Winston Churchill sent the first completed tripods with the British battalions deployed to the Eastern Front. Our forces stabilise Czar Nicholas II on the Russian throne and reinforce our allies against the Central Powers, forcing the Germans to shift battalions from the Western Front to the Eastern.

"Sir," Quincey says. "Why am I here?"

M keeps his reply too soft for the prisoner's ears. "Your commanding officer has granted my request for your indefinite leave."

"Indefinite leave, when most of the Balkans are still in enemy hands?" Quincey's voice is lowered, but it's possible King Bernhard hears him, given he's pitching his words for the failing ears of a seventy-year-old mortal. "Why are you in Lutha, anyhow? What the devil's going on, Father?"

For the first time in my twenty-six years, Mycroft Holmes looks his age.

"Your mother has disappeared on an intelligence oper-ation," he whispers. "Your joint mission is to recover her."

I open my mouth to speak.

"Don't ask," M says. "Your mother must never meet Miss Stein."

Altstadt District, Lustadt, Lutha, 24 December 1916

Church bells ring across the city. Neighbours sing "Stille Nacht" as they light candles on the tallest fir in St. Bojan's Square and twine pine garlands around the lowest leg-segments of the nearby British tripod. Christmastide has never been so lean in Lustadt, I expect, or joy so great. It's two days since British forces ended the Austrian occupation of the capital of Lutha.

Under the noise, I hear a lively interpretation of Joplin's "Pine Apple Rag" from the town house I'm approaching. When my key clicks in the lock of the front door, the music stops. The silence gives way to footsteps before I can step into the hall.

The light of sunset rises like water on the slight form of the woman who descends the stairs from the first floor. The slanting beams reveal an evening dress in an elegant pre-war style and the youthful aspect of her delicate features. The light finds soft gold glints in the darkness of her pompadour.

It also reveals my missing coat and filthy skirt.

I frown at the woman. "Return to your spinet, Clarimal, and mask your ears from the carols and bells."

"Sacred sounds hardly trouble me now." She draws near, speaking English with an antique Austrian accent. "The war grinds on, and mortals increasingly fall away from God."

Bare months ago, she'd not have spoken the holy name, because doing so would have caused her so much pain.

Sacred sounds and objects have never affected me. As a dhampir, I possess a soul. Like my mortal mother, I have the chance of Heaven or Hell.

Mindful not to smear Clarimal's gown, I keep my body from brushing hers as we kiss.

She touches the side of my face. "I've sent my renfield to join the celebration, but there's nothing celebratory about your expression, darling. M must have cancelled your leave."

"You and I rescued the queen of Lutha," I say. "M keeps the king of Lutha hidden in the dungeon."

"And you've given him your coat." Clarimal slips her arm through mine as we proceed up the staircase. "King Bernhard is foreign-born," she observes. "M must want to verify the man wasn't serving the Central Powers."

"You're correct on every count," I say. "But M should secure the man who led the Luthanian Army personally in a comfortable location."

"The Austria of my childhood died long ago," Clarimal says. "My childhood died only when I understood the behaviour of empires."

"You speak of the Austrians and Germans," I say. "This is not *English* behaviour."

Clarimal studies my face. "It's not the reason M summoned you on your birthday," she says. "Do you need to eat before your mission?"

"I need only my Webley and the mountain-man's clothes I wore when I slipped into Lutha," I reply. "After leaving M, I ate at the palace mess."

7

My lover is unable to eat, gaining nourishment only from blood. A dhampir may eat like a mortal, though it's blood that heals me quickest from grave injury. Only a mortal's blood aids an *upiór* or dhampir who's risen from the dead.

"M doesn't want you to know any of this," I tell Clarimal. "But for the last month, my mother's been operating under-cover in the principality of Tann."

"A wild place," Clarimal says, "and the only part of Lutha still in enemy hands. And, if we may believe the old stories, Tann is home to an entrance to the Hollow Earth."

"If it is, Queen Emma failed to mention this detail of her birthplace."

"That would be rather a large piece of information to give to foreign agents." Clarimal's expression grows pensive. "We may be fortunate she could provide any information."

Before the fall of Lustadt, Clarimal and I searched for the missing royal couple, and found the queen in the control of the Austrians' puppet, Prince Peter of Blentz. When we spirited Queen Emma to safety, she didn't say what befell her in Blentz's power. Perhaps it was only captivity. But even the suggestion of defilement may ruin a woman's honour, so not even British intelligence knows we found King Barnhard's wife chained to Blentz's bed.

It's not for *my* sake that I conceal my bastardy.

As we enter my bedroom, Clarimal presses the back of my hand to her breast-bone.

"Has something happened to your mother, Lucy?"

"A week ago, she infiltrated the Castle Von der Tann," I say. "It's been three days since British intelligence last heard from her."

Clarimal exhales. "M's sending you to rescue Mrs Holmes."

"Or recover her body."

I slam open my wardrobe.

Clarimal begins lighting the candles on my dressing table, though our eyes are no more affected by evening gloom than a cat's. "I'll go with you."

I place my men's wool socks and mountaineer's boots near the bench of my dressing table, then meet her gaze. "M has explicitly barred you from this mission."

Her black eyes are sharp as volcanic glass. "M's never mentioned his wife in my presence. He's the reason I've never met your mother and brothers, isn't he?"

Your mother must never meet Miss Stein. M has told me this many times, since I rejoined British intelligence at the start of the war, and Clarimal Stein joined with me. *Your mother must never meet Miss Stein.*

"My mother has been a vampire hunter almost since my birth," I remind Clarimal. "With her heightened senses, she would recognise your true nature as an *upiór*."

Wilhelmina Murray Harker Holmes believes the old folk-tale that vampires are naught but emotionless killing machines. Once, I told her this is false. She became so extraordinarily upset, I could only be grateful M didn't overhear.

Clarimal gives me a grim smile. "Given how long she's served British intelligence, your mother would recognise my true identity as Mircalla, Countess Karnstein. If M wants me never to meet her, it means he's not told her I also serve the Secret Intelligence Service."

I toss my grey felt Tyrolean hat on the dressing table, then pull the men's loden coat from my wardrobe and drape it over the back of the nearby chair.

I face my lover. "If my mother had only a mortal's normal senses, she would still realise what we are to one another."

"You don't wish to distress her with knowledge of our sin."

"Ah, Clarimal." I fling my men's shirt and trousers over the coat. "My mother blames herself for Dracula's assaults, though she never sought them. She doesn't desire women, either, but she'd blame herself for bequeathing me degeneracy."

As I remove my jacket and the shoulder holster with my Browning Short, Clarimal realises I've closed the subject and turns her attention to my skirt.

It's our habit to help one another to dress and undress. Such assistance has effects which cannot elude detection by our inhuman senses. By the time she's slipping off my silk stockings, I'm grinding my teeth.

"Even fear for my mother's life cannot prevent desire, it seems."

Clarimal smiles at our frustration and slides my men's shirt over my shoulders. "I cannot believe these garments persuade anyone you're a man, even when you bind your breasts."

"Perhaps men's clothes fool someone a mile away." I know she's trying to distract me from a ferocity of concern barely mastered by Holmes discipline, and I'm grateful. "It's not efficient to tramp through wildwood and mountain in a dirndl," I add, as I reach for the dark wool trousers. "And I expect my family wouldn't want me rescuing my mother in not a scrap of clothes."

Clarimal's lips twitch. "You've always been a naturist at heart, darling."

She knows of my childhood adventures as a sort of wild animal stalking other wild animals, discarding clothes to hone my hunting skills on remote moors and mountains in Yorkshire.

"Why should I like hampering myself with layers of clothing?" I'm adjusting the braces of my trousers. "Blood-drinkers don't share mortals' sensitivity to extremes of weather or temperature."

Clarimal laughs. "I never fought my attraction to women, but in hundreds of years of soullessness, I've not shaken off the strictures of a Catholic girlhood."

I reach for the gun-belt which hangs on my chair, weighted with an occupied holster and full ammunition pouch. "One irreligious savage in the household is sufficient, surely."

My smile fades as I examine my Webley Mk VI revolver. Finding all in order, I holster the loaded handgun. After buckling the belt round my waist, I seat myself before the mirror and reach for the agate drops clipped to my earlobes.

"Would you braid my hair?"

"Of course, darling." Clarimal unpins my hat, then removes the agate-topped stick from my chignon, spilling black waves down my back. "You've said your brothers' senses are nearly as heightened as your mother's," she remarks, reaching for my boar bristle hair-brush. "Why, then, hasn't M mentioned keeping me away from your brothers?"

"Because they're not vampire hunters?" I smile at her in the mirror. "Or, perhaps, because Quincey is a ladies' man?"

"A ladies' man?" Clarimal says. "You've told me Quincey's twenty years old and looks like Sherlock Holmes."

"With ginger hair." I reach for my socks. "I thought I must have been precocious, seducing another student at fifteen. But Quincey was thirteen when I realised I must supply him with sheaths, and an explanation of their proper use and function."

"Tod und Teufel." Clarimal's voice is amused. "Should we chance to meet, I'll endeavour to resist his masculine charms."

"Countess Karnstein, succumb to a man's charms?" I say. "That would be a first." My smile fades. "I asked for you, but M is sending Quincey with me on the mission."

At Clarimal's silence, I look up from the laces of my ankle-boot to find a line between her brows.

"Is Quincey an intelligence operative?"

"I haven't been informed," I say. "But almost every military pilot is."

"He heard M's refusal?" Clarimal asks. As I nod, she takes a hair ribbon from a drawer of the table. "Have you mentioned me to your brothers?"

"I have not, and of course Quincey asked who you were, once we'd left M's presence. I said you were a fellow operative working with me in Lutha and that I didn't know why M forbade your inclusion."

"Whatever M says, I should go with you."

"And ensure my mother realises we're lovers? Anyway," I say, "it's not practical. You sleep in a coffin."

Clarimal gently tugs my braid, signaling she's finished. "Rescuing your mother is more important than my comfort."

"'Comfort'?"

I rise so abruptly, she steps back.

"I remember when you were deprived of your coffin for three days." That was when we rescued Winston Churchill from Dr Krüger, the German science hero. "You experienced the torments of Hell!"

"The separation causes no permanent harm—"

"I won't have you suffer like that again." I realise I'm nearly shouting and force my voice low. "Even without your coffin, Clarimal, you fall asleep at dawn and remain insensible till midday. Quincey and I may not even reach the Castle Von der Tann by sunrise—"

The long-case clock on the landing chimes the quarter hour.

I pull on my men's coat so it covers my braid and give Clarimal a reassuring smile. "I'm supposed to meet my brother at the western gate of the Altstadt in fifteen minutes."

As she shakes her head doubtfully, I remember the night I sought her on the *Titanic* with an ash-wood stake, and abruptly crush her to me.

"A farewell, darling?" she whispers. "Or a premonition?"

"Dhampirs are as immune to premonitions as *upióry*." I suppress a shiver. "Sometimes, I remember I almost destroyed you, because I falsely believed vampires had no emotions and did only evil."

"Why wouldn't you believe that," she says, "when both priests and philosophers teach it?"

"Why have scientists not learned the truths of vampire behaviour, when they've plumbed the truths of human behaviour?"

"Have they?" Clarimal says. "Lucy, you and your brother will be greatly outnumbered in Tann. And if Tann *is* home to a passage from the Hollow Earth, then Dr Krüger may be there."

"If Tann had such a passage, wouldn't Krüger have made his way back to Germany months ago?" I say. "I think he died when I trapped him in the German passage to the centre of the earth."

Clarimal frowns. "Dr Krüger escaped the *Titanic*. His inventions dwarf those of Edison and Tesla. We cannot assume he died. I should go with you to Tann—"

"You know that's impossible." I brush a loose lock of gilt-bronze hair from her face. "Don't worry. Quincey Holmes isn't a normal mortal, and I haven't forgotten the information Queen Emma gave us about secret passages in the Castle Von der Tann. My brother and I shall have our mother safe in Lustadt before you've slept twice."

My lover's frown deepens.

Black Mountains, Principality of Tann, Lutha, 25 December 1916

"If I recall your words correctly," Quincey Holmes murmurs, "there should be no dead ends in the secret passages of the Castle Von der Tann."

"So Queen Emma informed me—but are we in the Castle Von der Tann?" I'm running my fingertips over the wall blocking our progress. "Feel this wall, and the walls on either side."

In the light of our battery-powered belt lamps, my half-brother brushes his fingers across each wall of the hidden passage we occupy.

"That's not fitted stone," he says. "We've passed into the living rock of the peak beneath the castle."

"I've found a peep-hole in the end wall." I bring my eye to the opening. "It's black as pitch on the other side—ah. Do you hear that?"

Quincey says, "I hear tumblers in a lock."

A lock clicks open, several yards beyond the wall. It's followed by the snap of a light switch.

I step back, blinking my dazzled eye, and my brother bends to the spy-hole.

He mutters, "How many bloody light bulbs *are* there on the other side of the wall?"

Through the opening comes a Wiesbaden accent, speaking cultured German. The voice is so harsh and distorted, I'm not sure whether it belongs to a man or a woman. The words are difficult to understand.

"You won't be alone with the captive," the damaged voice says. "My machine-man will accompany you and the captive to Pellucidar."

"I should hope it will." The second voice belongs to a high-born Luthanian man, and concludes with a laugh. "You've told me such vivid tales of man-eating dinosaurs and savage cave-men at the centre of the earth."

Quincey speaks to me softly. "I can't see much, but I'm looking into a cave. The voices are coming from behind a pile of stones against the wall. Your vision must be recovered." He steps back. "Have a dekko and tell me what you see."

My half-brothers' senses are keener than those of any mortal save our mother, but not a match for mine.

"Two men are coming into sight from behind the rubble pile," I say. "And I hear the footsteps of a third individual."

"By the sounds," Quincey murmurs, "that one weighs as much as three stout men and wears metal shoes."

"I recognize the man who's dressed like us. He's Lt Adalbert Maenck, a Luthanian cavalry officer who turned traitor and aided the Austrians."

"What of the other?"

"He's immensely tall and broad-shouldered, and wears the uniform of a lieutenant colonel of the Imperial German Army."

Quincey says, "We'd see German officers sometimes in the trenches around Lustadt."

"Did you see an officer whose uniform is made of black leather, and whose head is hidden by a mask which resembles a stovepipe, closed to a point at the top?"

Quincey inhales. "You're describing the Steel Mask."

"It seems G-8's report of Herr Stahlmaske's death was in error," I say. "Care to see his and Maenck's companion?"

Quincey takes my place at the peep-hole. "Dear God, it's an automaton, carrying someone wrapped in a blanket and tied in ropes!" He reaches for his Webley revolver. "Our mother—"

"—may not be their captive," I remind him.

But I've already opened the flap of my holster and resumed searching the end-wall for a latch.

"Let's hope she isn't," my brother mutters. "It's said the Steel Mask's injuries turned him into a sadic torturer."

"Or they unleashed his cruelty," I say. "Britain has no shortage of war invalids with face mutilations, but when one commits harm, it's to kill himself."

The spy-hole brings us Lt Maenck's amused tones.

"From everything you've told me, Mr Stahlmaske, I should have an *army* of Dr Krüger's machine-men to protect me at the earth's core."

Quincey stiffens. "I thought Krüger was dead."

Dr Krüger escaped the Titanic. His inventions dwarf those of Edison and Tesla. We cannot assume he died.

Stahlmaske's reply holds no amusement. "Maenck, you jest as merrily as Rupert of Hentzau," he says. "But Hentzau died in an endeavour considerably less hazardous than transporting a prisoner across primeval wilderness at the centre of the earth."

"More Hollow Earth rot," Quincey mutters.

My fingers find a hidden latch. There's a small click and lines of light appear, outlining a stone-faced door in the wall. Quincey and I extinguish our belt lamps and listen for a reaction to the click.

In the cave, the footsteps recede without a pause. Water drips. Cool air seeps through the cracks and brings us the smells of minerals and mould and old bat *guano*.

"Mr Stahlmaske!" Maenck's voice rings with mock shock. "Have you forgotten I'm more motivated than Hentzau ever was? Your commanders promised me the kingship of Lutha if I get the vampire hunter alive to Dr Krüger."

"'Vampire hunter'?" Quincey reaches precipitously for the secret door.

"Patience, or we'll do our mother only harm." I speak as if I've not begun trembling, like a thoroughbred at the start line of the Royal Ascot. "If she's killed, no quantity of my blood can bring her back to life."

Quincey steps aside, and I slowly open the door. It doesn't make a sound. Queen Emma's family kept the hinges well-oiled.

Quincey looks over my shoulder, unwittingly rousing my old irritation that he gained six inches on my height of six feet.

"Dear God," he breathes. "That cave could swallow a dozen aëroplanes comfortably."

The cavern is dark near the walls, but the rest of the space is illuminated by the hundreds of electric bulbs strung among the stalactites. Maenck and Stahlmaske shut off their belt lamps as they emerge from the shadows and start up the rise in the floor. The mechanical man follows them, carrying their blanket-wrapped captive up the underground ridge.

"We can't shoot at the men when they're crowded so close to our mother," I say softly to Quincey. "And we shan't be slipping from one stalagmite to another to reach them."

"I daresay we won't. Stalagmites ring most of the cave, but they've been removed from the floor everywhere else."

The detached stalagmites are piled with boulders and rubble against the wall, several yards to our right. Sharp edges show that the calcite formations were broken recently. The rock pile rises higher than our heads and looks unstable.

I tell Quincey, "We'll watch for clean shots at the men." I tilt my head at the crest of the ridge. "You'll have already noticed the motor-lorries."

Both lorries have *camouflage* streaks of dull green and grey and red-brown on their metal bodies and the canvas roofs of their beds. The closer lorry leans down the slope, revealing a steering wheel on the left and a pair of bench-style seats under the metal roof. In the centre of each front seat, a Martian-style heat-ray device is fixed, its muzzle jutting between the panes of the wind-screen.

The Germans gained the heat-ray technology from England through my failure on the *Titanic*.

"There's no smell of petrol or Diesel fumes," Quincey observes grimly. "We shall hope those lorries burn alcohol, like other Austrian and German motor vehicles."

British tripods and leg-lorries are powered by the remarkable engine which our scientists recently "reverse engineered" from the technology of the failed Martian invasion of 1902—technology the Central Powers should not possess.

I say, "I'm not feeling optimistic, given those lorries have legs."

"They've clawed arms in front, instead of Martian-style tentacles like our leg-lorries," Quincey says. "But it's clear some bloody traitor or spy has compromised British secrets."

"Whoever's responsible, they didn't build those leg-lorries here."

I tilt my head towards the far wall.

It's in shadow no mortal eye should pierce, but Quincey says, "I see the mouth of another cave, or a natural tunnel. The mouth's more than big enough to admit a lorry. It's guarded by two automata armed with machine-rifles, one on either side."

My mother's mortal sons have abilities almost the equal of hers. I suspect it's explained by Dr Watson's hypothesis of the miscarriages she's suffered since Arthur's birth. I was eavesdropping when the good doctor told my mother that bearing a vampire's child must have altered the environment of her womb, making it increasingly hostile to conception with a mortal man. As a selfish eight-year-old, I'd hoped I'd made it impossible for my mother to give my stepfather more children. I couldn't conceive of the sorrow that would cause them.

I suppose I don't quite understand it yet. I've never wanted children, and if I did, I'd still not have them. They might be dhampirs. I know what it's like, growing up a dhampir among mortals.

Near the crest of the rise, Maenck is gesturing at the leg-lorries and Stahlmaske's automaton.

"Peculiar as they look," Maenck says, "you can't help admiring Dr Krüger's machines."

"Dr Krüger's lobster-lorries and machine-men are both impressive, but in short supply at present," Stahlmaske tells him. "My machine-man must suffice to guard you in Pellucidar."

"What the devil is Pellucidar, anyway?" my brother mutters.

I show him a humourless smile. "The world inside the Hollow Earth."

Quincey's eyes widen. "You've been there?"

I return my attention to our foes. "Krüger's been there."

"One machine-man, when this cave alone has three?" Maenck says to Stahlmaske. "But—"

Maenck turns towards the automaton behind them and pulls the blanket off the captive's head.

Quincey starts forward and I seize his shoulder. "Hold."

"—what if the vampire hunter wakes?" Maenck asks Stahlmaske. "I've heard Mrs Holmes heals faster than other mortals. And you've said she's stronger than any man." His smile widens. "Surely I need more protection!"

"If Mrs Holmes wakes, a blow from your pistol-butt will knock her senseless again," Stahlmaske says. "But she shouldn't." A note of satisfaction enters his voice as he adds, "I wounded her nearly unto death."

"That brute—" Quincey lunges against my grip.

I tighten my hand with force enough to break a normal mortal's bones. "They'll kill you before you get three steps into the light. My blood can't resurrect you, either."

Stahlmaske looks at his mechanical. "Machine-man, secure the prisoner in the front passenger seat of the nearer lorry, then sit on the back bench."

I feel the tension in Quincey's muscles as the mechanical man buckles a belt round our mother's waist.

The belt is attached to the seat, like the belts in British leg-lorries and tripods and the aëroplanes of our Royal Flying Corps.

"I've no experience with automata," Quincey mutters. "Is there any bloody way to stop the things?"

"I fought some of Dr Krüger's mechanicals in Germany last February," I say. "They were incapacitated only when I crushed their crania and the electrodes within."

As Stahlmaske's mechanical steps back, Maenck gestures at their captive. "If the lobster breaks down," he remarks, "at least I'll have pleasant company."

Stahlmaske says, "Leave the woman untouched and hasten to Dr Krüger—if you want to become King of Lutha."

"Spoilsport," Maenck says. "*You* got to play with her."

My brother convulses against my grip, and his boot strikes a loose stone, sending it cracking into another rock.

Stiffening, Maenck and Stahlmaske reach for the Lugers on their belts and turn around.

My brother and I are already leaping for the shadows of the stalagmites near the rock pile.

Bullets whistle around us, and ricochets whine.

Alighting, I raise my Webley in my right hand and look back at Quincey. "Hit?"

"No." We speak softly, reading lips, although the gunfire must have set the men's ears ringing as loudly as ours. "Were you?"

"No."

The mechanical men guarding the passage to the earth's core have little horns on the sides of their heads. They would have heard the gunfire. Both remain motionless, their infantrymen's machine-rifles at port arms as they stare straight ahead.

Stahlmaske and Maenck are peering in the direction of the sound Quincey made. Their Lugers are raised, indicating they haven't emptied the weapons. Their left hands fumble for the switches of their belt lamps.

The temptation to shoot directly at the men is enormous, but I cannot risk it. My mother is behind Stahlmaske and his mechanical. If either moves as I fire, I might kill her.

My shot echoes like thunder and the muzzle flash is blinding, but I hear a metallic crash and wrathful cry through the ringing of my ears.

My vision clears, and I see my bullet struck its target. The stalactite broke and plunged down, striking the mechanical and Stahlmaske. The mechanical lies motionless, its steel cranium crushed beneath the stalactite. Stahlmaske is holding his damaged right shoulder with his left hand. Where his Luger has gone, I cannot see. I don't see Maenck, either.

"There's some ringing in my ears," Quincey says, "but I think I hear a new sound—"

"A keyed ignition switch," I say. "Maenck's got in the lorry with our mother—"

Green smoke pours from the leg-lorry's exhaust pipe.

I suppress a curse. "They've stolen the secret of our Martian engines."

Stahlmaske turns on his belt lamp. Its light sweeps past us and returns.

"There—two of the vampire hunter's monstrous get," he shouts. "Burn them, Maenck."

German agents have descriptions of my appearance. Quincey is betrayed by his resemblance to our famous uncle. But no foe of England should know my half-brothers have more-than-mortal abilities.

Maenck reacts to Stahlmaske's command by raising the lorry to a height of five feet on its spidery striding-legs.

Stahlmaske glances over his shoulder. "What the hell are you waiting for, Maenck? Turn the lobster about and incinerate the monsters with your heat-ray."

The lorry strides forward, taking our mother from behind Stahlmaske.

He flings himself down as Quincey and I fire.

As the echoes die, Stahlmaske's voice comes from a dip in the floor where he's dropped out of sight. "Maenck!"

"It gives me sorrow," Maenck replies, "but keeping you alive isn't my mission. My mission is getting Mrs Holmes alive to Dr Krüger. But fear not, Stahlmaske—you have twice as many machine-men to keep *you* safe."

The lorry scuttles towards the passage to the earth's core. My mother bobs limply in her bonds and seat belt, concealing and revealing Maenck erratically until the lorry enters the tunnel.

Stahlmaske's voice rises. "Machine-men, kill the intruders near the rock pile."

Quincey and I leap into the shelter of the rock pile before the mechanicals can fire. Bullets strike stalagmites and ricochet around us in a spray of shards. The mechanicals keep firing, as if intent on emptying the magazines of their Schouboe machine-guns.

"Machine-men," cries Stahlmaske, "hold your damned fire until you've advanced and found your targets!"

The mechanicals cease firing and start noisily forward at an astonishing pace for their weight.

We're not out of sight of the mortal. His light-beam locates Quincey and me among the stalagmites, and something strikes my left hip like a mallet and shatters the joint. Then I hear the shot that's crippled me.

"It's no damn use ducking," Churchill used to tell his men, when a German gun cracked on the Western Front. "The bullet has gone a long way past by now."

Before we can return fire, Stahlmaske's lowered his head, Luger, and lamp out of sight.

Prone beside me, Quincey says, "You're hit."

"Get back to M and tell him to keep the Royal Flying Corps from bombing the Castle Von der Tann, if he wants to see his wife again. I'll recover our mother and kill Krüger."

"How on earth do you expect to accomplish that feat, alone and injured?"

In truth, I probably need my brother's aid.

And Clarimal's with it.

"I've piloted British leg-lorries—"

"Lucy, you can't even walk at the moment." Quincey sets his jaw, stubborn as Sherlock Holmes. "I'm staying."

"A bomb might trap us all in the passage, unable to escape before you and Mother die. You will obey my order, Lt Holmes."

His eyes narrow. "I'll be back with reinforcements."

I smile. "As I expect. Now go, before every Austrian in the castle arrives to investigate the gunfire."

Quincey returns his weapon to his holster. Then he seizes my free hand in both his hands and wrings it.

"Don't fall on any stakes, sister."

"Merry Christmas to you, as well, brother."

Then he's returning to the secret passage at an inhuman pace. I holster my Webley and crawl to the rock pile.

Stahlmaske's lamp-beam reappears, eventually locating me where I've pulled myself part way up the pile and begun tugging on a rock.

"I'll fill your heart with lead, dhampir," he calls, "and make sure you stay dead."

As his Luger cracks, the boulder comes loose. It crashes down, loosing more rocks, which send others cascading. The noise becomes a roar.

By the time I push away the rocks covering my body, the mechanical men are buried without a trace.

I crawl across the floor until I can see Stahlmaske in his bolt-hole. He's lying on his back, pinned beneath a boulder which landed yards from my avalanche. The boulder's left his limbs free, but it must have broken most of the bones in his torso.

Stahlmaske raises his head and sees me slowly approaching in the light of the ceiling bulbs. He aims his Luger at me with his left hand. The angle of the floor tilts his body so the light enters the eye-holes of his mask. His eyes appear crimson.

"You look uncomfortable," I call in German.

"Stop, monster," he shouts, "or I'll shoot."

It's possible he still has bullets in his Luger.

"Fire," I say, "if you want to stay trapped in this cave."

Stahlmaske keeps his aim on me, but doesn't fire.

I drag myself closer with my functioning hand and leg. My left arm is shattered. Blood flows from the reopened wound in my hip and the new bullet hole in my side. Blood slides from the places where falling rocks cut wool and linen and tore skin and muscle. My hat is lost under the avalanche. When the ends of my broken bones grate together, the sensation stops my breath. Blood swells my abdomen, and a growing pressure on my chest makes my breaths increasingly shallow. When I cough, my vision darkens, and I spray blood.

Stahlmaske's raised arm wavers. My ears are ringing too much to hear his pulse or respiration, but I don't need to. His scent heralds the approach of death.

As does mine.

"We've made a lot of noise," Stahlmaske says. "The Austrians will be here directly. I'll tell them not to destroy you, dhampir, if you agree to free me."

"I agree to free you."

He lowers his handgun.

I drive the base of my fist into his mask, snapping his head sideways and denting the metal.

My vision darkens, but I find breath enough to speak.

"Freedom has many meanings."

I pull the mask from the mortal's head. He has eyelids, lowered in unconsciousness, but rumour and British intelligence are both correct. Stahlmaske's skull has been burned mostly naked.

I think of the destruction the Steel Mask has wrought on the British Expeditionary Force and our allies. I think of the women and children he has maimed and slain in his own country. I contemplate my odds of rescuing my mother and defeating Dr Krüger if the Steel Mask reports recent events to the Austrians.

I've vowed never to kill save where it's necessary.

I sink my fangs in the scarred flesh of Stahlmaske's neck and drink him dry.

Pellucidar

After twelve hours of travel through the passage, the odometer reveals I've come five hundred miles.

Moments later, a boulder falls from the ceiling.

As I brake, several near-naked figures drop into the light of the head and side lamps.

"Smashing," I say *sotto voce*, drawing my sidearm. "I'm being ambushed by cave-men."

Fifteen men and four women with mortal scents surround the "lobster" and point their spears and rifles at me. A fifth woman is trotting up the passage with a rifle in one hand and a pole in the other. The pole would serve adequately in shifting a boulder.

The mortals' firearms are a mix of muzzle-loading muskets of unknown origin and breech-loading rifles of German, American, and English makes. A hirsute man of massive build and the woman with the pole each have a Rigby Nitro Express rifle. It's an English elephant gun, and it has a mule kick the woman appears too slender to withstand.

The hirsute man fixes his double barrels on me and shouts in German. "Kapitulieren Sie!"

I replace my revolver in my holster and raise my hands. "Ich gebe auf, mein Herr."

The mortals look about twenty years old. The men are bearded and wear fur loin-clouts, while the women wear sleeveless fur tunics, open like ponchos at the sides. Both sexes wear stout belts equipped with sheathed knives, looped ropes, and battery-powered lamps, as well as a barbaric *mélange* of ornaments: claw and fang, ivory and bronze, silver and gold. The woman with the pole also wears amber and pearls and dentalium shells. She and the German speaker have Colt revolvers holstered at their belts.

I've long since cast off my loden coat. The electric lamp on the instrument panel exposes the dried blood on the white linen of my shirt, and the smooth skin beneath its tears and bullet hole. Does the conjunction of blood and vanished injuries make them wonder if I'm a blood-drinker?

The hirsute rifleman speaks again in his curiously accented German. "Put your machine-insect to sleep, miss, and raise your arms again."

Levers lower the lobster nearly to the ground. The key shuts off the engine and the lamps.

A blood-drinker's eyes adjust to changes in light levels more quickly than a human's, but the mortals ignite their belt lamps without haste. My captors believe I'm as mortal as they.

Some fifty yards ahead, a blot of illumination suggests the passage ends in sunlight.

Sunlight, at the centre of the earth?

It's been more than a day since I last slept. That doesn't affect me as it would a mortal, but it can dull my awareness, even in situations less monotonous than travelling through an endless cave. I've not noticed branches in the natural tunnel—but have I missed a fork, and returned to the surface?

The German speaker says, "Get out of the machine-insect, miss."

"Yes, sir." Slowly, I remove the driving gauntlets I found in the glove-box. Keeping my attention on the German speaker, I unbuckle my seat belt and open my door. Then I raise my hands and step out of the lorry.

The mortals have dark skin, eyes, and hair. They might be Indo-European, but they're no race I know. The woman with the pole and four of the men have the aquiline features of red Indians. If you ignore the scars and occasional missing eye or digit or hand, the twenty range in appearance from pleasant to stunning.

Standing close to attractive people in a state of undress has a predictable effect on my libido.

The woman with the pole narrows her eyes, studying my face more closely in the glow of the belt lamps, then smiles with great amusement. Most mortals have senses hardly sharper than a spoon, but I've met an English lord with a nose as keen as an ape's. If the lovely lass shares his faculty, she's the most dangerous of my formidable captors.

The hirsute man addresses me. "Lower your arms, miss, but don't resist."

He gestures at the amused woman. She hands her pole and rifle to a nearby man, then takes the revolver from my holster and slips it in her belt. Still smiling, she steps behind me.

I consider how easily she might slip the blade of her knife into my heart.

She pulls my arms behind my back and secures my wrists, making the bonds tight but not painful. She's as tall as Quincey, but she leans towards me as she fastens the other end of her grass rope in a slack noose around my neck. She forms the knot swiftly despite the missing pair of fingers at the outer edge of her left hand.

Her breath brushes my ear. Her scent alters, and her respiration and heartbeat grow more rapid. She finds me desirable, or enjoys the act of confining another.

She speaks very softly.

"Do you understand English?"

I risk a faint "Yes."

"I'm An the Mezop."

I whisper, "I'm Luzia Holm."

The German speaker says, "An."

An the Mezop reclaims her rifle, then closes her maimed hand on the length of rope between my wrists and neck. The noose presses against my throat with not quite enough force to cause discomfort. She judges her grip finely.

Gesturing to his followers, the German speaker tells me, "We leave the passage now."

We approach the cave mouth at a healthy pace. An stays at my side, retaining her grip on my leash. Her right hand holds the express rifle as lightly as a willow switch. The other mortals surround us, their eyes alert as they keep their rifles and spears pointed at me. No one seems to notice how poorly their garments maintain their modesty.

No one speaks. No one jabs or strikes or spits on me. No one disturbed the lobster, though they must have found it tempting, and the carbine and Luger on the front seat, as well.

These humans are disciplined, however wild they look, and they were waiting for me. Is this because they saw Maenck's lobster come through the tunnel, and prepared themselves for the possibility of more lorries? Or is it because they serve Krüger?

As An and I step through the mouth of the passage, I stop with an oath. "Lieber Gott!"

Beyond a wide stone ledge, sunlit wilderness spreads. Lines of trees wander a plain, marking the flow of rivers with a primeval beauty. In places, grassland gives way to rocky hills or lush forest, and in the distance, a vast lake spreads. I'm looking upon a peninsula so large, the islands of the surrounding sea must be almost invisible to mortal eyes.

The grasslands are populated with herds which must each hold a thousand animals or more. The air teems with commensurate flocks. I recognise many of the nearest flying creatures. Most went extinct on the surface thousands or millions of years ago.

I've not felt such wonder at the sight of a new land, even when setting foot on the primordial plateau of Maple White Land.

I might fancy I've traveled through time to pre-Adamic Eden, if the illusion weren't dashed by the device receding across the plain. It moves at an extraordinarily steady pace, drawing a diagonal wake of flattened grass from the mountain I stand upon.

I mutter, "Maenck—"

A large creature bursts into sight beyond the lip of the ledge.

Beside me, An the Mezop points at the living fossil and says, "Thipdar."

Tilting its head, the pterodactyl sweeps its gaze across the ledge as it climbs the sky. It's covered with long grey hairs and has a twenty-foot wing-span, like the pterodactyls I encountered at Dr Krüger's German headquarters. Those pterodactyls were servants of a winged reptilian called a Mahar, an intelligent ally of Krüger's that came from inside the earth.

Does this pterodactyl serve Krüger?

I look about, but see no Mahars or additional pterodactyls.

There's something else I don't see.

"Why is the horizon so far away that I cannot find it?" I mutter.

My lovely captor whispers, "What's a 'horizon'?"

I gasp as I understand.

I shall never find the horizon, for the interior of the earth curves upward on every side, until it disappears in the thickness of atmosphere.

And I see this because a swollen sun occupies the heart of the vast hollow at the centre of the earth.

Black as the Pit from pole to pole? I suppress a smile. The poet got it wrong, about the interior of the earth.

A voice comes to me, speaking English with a small-town Connecticut accent. "If she's Teutonic, I'm a Negro."

Turning to the voice, I face the four armed, nearly naked mortals I've already noticed peripherally on the left side of the ledge, where they've been awaiting my captors.

They're all strangers, but I recognise two from British intelligence dossiers. They're secret agents in the service of the neutral United States. The pair were presumed lost in an attempt to reach the earth's core with the older operative's experimental drilling vehicle.

The younger operative studies me with keen grey eyes, then answers his aged colleague in the accent of an upper-caste scion of New Haven. "She's a Turk, Abner."

In England, strangers typically assume my aquiline features are as Anglo-Saxon as those of Sherlock
Holmes. They miss or disregard my olive skin and the
shape and colour of my eyes. My natural father's mother
was Turcoman and his father was Attila the Hun. The
Kaiser's rumoured notion that the Huns were German
Aryans is fanciful indeed.

"David, my boy, I can distinguish the Oriental races,"
the older American tells the younger with amused indig-
nation. "She's a Eurasiatic from Austria-Hungary or the
Balkans."

An watches the Americans with an expression to
match my own, a look which suggests we're trying to
decipher the discussion and failing.

The coppery-skinned man towering beside the Americans has features more like An's than the racial tie can
explain. The beautiful woman standing close to David
has a family resemblance to the German speaker, who
is approaching the party. With intermittent use of the
English word "German," he addresses the four in a gut-
tural tongue I don't recognise, though I speak a dozen
languages and have heard dozens more.

The younger American studies me. "Wie heissen Sie,
Fräulein?"

I reply in a flawless upper-class Viennese accent.
"Luzia Holm, mein Herr."

"And what, Miss Holm," he says in German, "brings
a young woman to the centre of the earth?"

"I'm chasing my mother's kidnapper—"

"—in a stolen experimental vehicle?" David smiles.
"Abner and I know about Dr Krüger's Martian-style
trucks, and we know about the war between the Central

Powers and the Triple Entente. Also, the man who came through the tunnel before you told us he might have a pursuer or two."

"He knew Austria would send someone to recover their kidnapped intelligence agent."

"He identified his woman captive as an Allied spy," David replies.

"He's a liar, and a Luthanian working for the Allies," I lie. "If you got a good look at my mother, you cannot deny our relationship."

The last bit isn't a lie, though my facial features more closely resemble my natural father's.

"You look somewhat like Adalbert Maenck's captive," David says. "But even if you were her twin, Miss Holm—or whatever your name is—I can't risk letting you go free—"

A tremendous roar heralds the appearance of dinosaurs around the curve of the mountain. They're as big as polar bears and as nimble as mountain goats. Improbably, they're covered with feathers in brilliant shades of blue, yellow, and red. Counter-balanced by tapering tails, the beasts lean forward as they charge, extending tiny arms and vast jaws. Their far smaller size and the immense domes of their skulls indicate the creatures are Tylosteus ornatus, not Tyrannosaurus rex, but does that matter when a dozen charge you?

The mortals turn to face the dinosaurs, and I tense to break my bonds while they're distracted.

I feel a breath on my ear.

"The captive woman looked like you." An the Mezop's murmur comes to me clearly despite the bellow of dinosaurs and crack of rifles. "If you agree to help us kill the mountain-tyrannosaurs, I'll cut you free."

"I agree."

Her blade saws the rope. Her left hand slips into sight long enough to hang her lamp over my gun-belt. The hand reappears to holster my Webley.

"Your little gun may kill a little dinosaur," she says, "but it'll do no good against large beasts. Get the heat-ray."

The rope parts.

As I sprint for the passage, An empties both barrels of her Rigby into the throat of the closest Tylosteus, riding the kick easily.

I reach the lobster-lorry quickly, but the gunfire grows sporadic as I manoeuvre the machine over the boulder.

When the lobster reaches the ledge, An is reloading her Rigby with two great .470 cartridges from her bandoliers and smiling like a hunter eager to bag her first elephant.

Beyond her, six dinosaurs and three Cro-Magnons lie dead. The old American presses his back to the mountainside and aims his smoking revolvers at the Tylosteus reaching for him. The other five saurians surround the rest of the mortals. The young American grips his express rifle by the barrels and raises it like a club as the Cro-Magnons thrust bayonets and spears into the flesh of carnivores unslowed by the bullet wounds riddling their breasts and bellies.

The mortals are no friends of mine.

I halt the lobster and depress the switch atop the device beside me. It begins to hum. Beyond the windscreen, green smoke puffs from its muzzle.

An empties her elephant gun, and the dinosaur reaching for her kinsman collapses, its skull blown away by the double shot through its open jaws.

I depress the switch to a new setting. The hum deepens and green smoke streams from the muzzle. I swivel the lobster-body on its striding-legs like a machine-gun.

One by one, the heads of the surviving dinosaurs fall flaming from their necks.

Before the mortals can react, I shut off the invisible heat-ray and put the lorry in motion.

An leaps over the far door and seats herself on the other side of the device.

"What the devil are you doing?"

Her ears must be ringing from the noise of her elephant gun, but she reads my lips.

"You saved us, though we're enemies." She smiles at me over her rifle. "I'll help you save your mother."

If I pause to remove her from the cabin, the mortals might have time to kill or capture me.

"Fasten your lap belt like mine or you'll bounce out the window."

She's barely got the strap buckled when I send the lobster over the edge of the ledge—

—onto a slope steep enough to stop the heart of a mountain goat.

"Hold on," I shout as I turn the steering wheel.

An grins and keeps her hands on her rifle.

I slow the lobster, but the body tilts alarmingly as I turn the vehicle on the precipitous slope. Despite the seat belts, my hip slides into the heat-ray device and An's hip slams into the door. Her lamp and Stahlmaske's unsecured Luger fall through her window. If its gyroscopes and couplings and Martian-style "muscles" fail to prevent the lobster from tumbling down the mountain, neither of us will survive, and only one of us will resurrect.

An laughs.

I say, "Are you suicidal?"

She looks at me, her grin widening.

Then the lobster comes upright as I send it straight across the slope towards a line of trees.

The metal claws ring on the mountainside and dislodge loose rocks, startling markhors and marmots and a massive sabre-toothed cat with the coat of a Himalayan ounce. Birds and insects and deer burst onto the bare slope as the lobster crashes through the evergreens and bracken lining a beck. Slowing the vehicle to a quiet walk, I begin following the narrow gill down the mountainside.

As An reloads her express rifle, a muscle flexes like a steel band along her forearm.

She glances in my direction, and I say, "You should get on the floor, where the metal will shield you. No one can see us here, but someone can fire into the trees—"

"No one's going to shoot at Ja's cousin." She laughs. "I have never known such fun!"

Her eyes are alight, her lips parted in a smile of unself-conscious joy. The hair piled on her head catches a stray sunbeam and gleams like a raven's wing. She has the erect posture of a career soldier and the athletic grace ascribed to the young Irene Adler.

An is very beautiful.

I focus on my piloting. "Your friends won't like you helping me."

"They wouldn't like having their mothers abducted," she says. "David made an agreement with Dr Krüger. I haven't. And neither have you."

I meet her appraising gaze.

"I cannot tell you more. But I can stop the machine-insect and let you out any time you want."

She smiles slowly, looking me up and down. "Not yet."

My desire strengthens, for all I've no interest in an ignorant cave-girl. I'm relieved the lobster commands all my attention as the ravine deepens abruptly.

"Can you give me some idea where I am, besides 'on a mountain'?"

An's laugh is melodious. "You're descending the highest peak of the Mountains of the Clouds."

"Is your cave here?"

"You're from far away, if you think any Mezop lives in these mountains," she says with another laugh. "We live on islands and build our homes."

Our view is limited by trees and rocks on every side, but she gestures to our left—east, if I may trust the compass affixed to the instrument panel.

"I'm from Luana, the greatest island in the Lural Sea or any other." Lowering her arm, she considers me. "You won't find Dr Krüger at sea, or in the Mountains of the Clouds."

"Where can he be found?"

"At his factory. I've been there, with Ja and David and Abner." She points to our right, where the view is equally occluded. "Krüger's factory is beyond the Sojar Sea, beside the Great Peak. It's not one of the Mountains of the Cloud, but stands near the Land of Awful Shadow. Once we're off this mountain, I'll take you there."

"How far away is Krüger's factory?"

"How far?" She shrugs. "As many sleeps as it takes."

The air warms as the slope grows less steep, and the pines and firs mingle increasingly with oaks. Acorns the width of my palm leave me grateful for the cabin roof. One must deliver a cracking blow if it falls on your head.

Leaves rustle in a gust. Birds sing on every side. The beck grows wider and noisier as other brooks join its wandering course.

"Is your cousin the tall man who stood next to David?"

An nods. "Ja is my mother's sister's son and was once chief of the Mezops of Anoroc Island," she says. "Now he is—" she frowns "—king. My brother—he is home—is king of Luana Island."

I suppress a smile at assigning such elevated rank to Cro-Magnons.

"Did David or Abner make them kings?"

"Oh, David says all the chiefs in the alliance which he and Ja and some other chiefs have made are kings now," An says, "because they're part of an 'empire.' But how is the empire an alliance, when the chiefs take orders from David?"

Are David and Abner organizing local tribes to serve the United States—or their own ambitions?

"Is David a king?"

An gives me a shrewd look. "He calls himself the Emperor of the Federated Kingdoms of Pellucidar."

"Emperor of the whole world?"

"Just a part of it, but he says more human tribes will join the alliance so we can kill off all the Mahars."

She speaks with the serene certainty of a surface mortal discussing the necessity of annihilating all blood-drinkers or of a colonial official discussing the necessity of massacring the Pithecanthropi of Maple White Land.

"David and Abner didn't know what Mahars were, once," An says, "so maybe you don't, either. The Mahars are a race of intelligent flying reptiles."

I encountered a Mahar at Krüger's lair in Germany. The Mahar resembled the rhamphorhynchus, a prehistoric species similar to the pterodactyl. Unlike the rhamphorhynchi known to palaeontology, the Mahar was covered with feathers and had a wingspan of almost thirty feet.

"Why do you want to kill all Mahars?"

"Why would we not?" An asks in astonishment. "They eat gilaks—humans. The Mahars of Phutra used to fatten mainlanders like Thurian lidi and eat them. My cousin and I saw it more than once."

I slew Krüger's Mahar when it attempted to eat me.

"Is that why your tribe and Ja's joined David's alliance?"

"Ja's tribe joined because David is his friend. But they used force to make my tribe join the empire." Her eyebrows draw together. "That's not how an alliance should work."

"Is Dr Krüger in the alliance?"

"Krüger has his own alliance, with the human tribe of the mountain near his factory, and a city of feathered Mahars."

A city, in this savage land?

Then I remember something Krüger told me, months ago. *The Mahars have a great civilisation inside the earth.*

"David made a treaty between his alliance and Krüger's alliance," An continues, "because Krüger's factory makes things David and Abner's factories don't, and their factories make things Krüger's factory doesn't."

"Cosy," I say. "What does Krüger's factory make?"

"Machine-insects, bullets, bombs, and flying machines."

When we met in Germany, Krüger claimed to be building a factory for automated monoplanes, but British intelligence found no evidence of its existence. Krüger also spoke of visiting the interior of the earth. Why didn't I realise he might build the factory there?

An says, "Krüger hasn't agreed to trade any of these things to David yet." Her eyes narrow. "Once, David agreed we should kill all Mahars. Now, he says we mustn't attack Krüger's feathered Mahars. Krüger claims they don't eat humans, like the lizard-skinned Mahars do." She smiles without humour. "I think David might be too trusting of Krüger."

"I think you might be right."

The slope is leveling, the oaks giving way to tropical trees. The boles are more widely spaced, and the floor of the forest is hidden by moss and decaying leaves. The gloom and openness suggest the interior of an ancient cathedral at dusk. The forest aisles hold no shape or shadow of animal life, but there is no silence. I glance up.

Twined with vines as thick as my wrist and layered with fungi as wide as book-shelves, the boles soar. Far above, the branches are laden with glossy leaves and brilliant with orchids and passion flowers and scores of blooms I cannot name. The interwoven boughs are as crowded as a high street at midday, but the traffic are monkeys and squirrels and serpents and tree-frogs and parrots and innumerable other species. The air is full of squawks and peeps and shrieks, and the roars and howls of unseen beasts of frightful lung capacity.

"Even the Amazon jungle wasn't like this." I realise I'm speaking softly, as if in church. "I've never seen a place so full of wildlife."

An stares at me. "There is such abundance anyplace without snow."

I remember an older friend's remark about her childhood—*Father's hunting parties at Elveden would shoot thousands of birds in a day*—and am plunged into surprising melancholy.

An gestures. "This stream becomes a river that flows to the Sojar Sea. We can follow the river to the coast and the coast to the Great Peak, or we can travel straight across the plain to Dr Krüger's factory."

"Is it safer to follow the water?"

"Both ways are dangerous," she says indifferently. "Crossing the plain is direct."

I bring the lobster to the western edge of the trees. Halting in the shadow of a tree fern, I raise the lobster until its legs are nearly straight, and An laughs in delight. Her merriment swells as I swivel the lobster-body slowly from north to south, as if panning with a cinematic camera, so we may more fully survey the plain.

I nearly laugh myself, at the vista of brontosaurs and triceratopses and mastodons and hundreds of other species which vanished from the earth's surface long ago. In all my time in Maple White Land, I saw far fewer primeval species.

Most of the visible beasts are grass-eaters. The sight should offer little comfort, when a stampeding aurochs or iguanodon may be no less deadly than a starving tiger.

But the sight of innumerable dangerous beasts from the dawn of time only fills me with delight.

I haven't forgotten my mother.

"We've followed the stream too far," I tell An. "I cannot see Maenck's machine-insect—"

"We don't need to see it." She points west, where the mountains recede into the rising distance. "To reach Krüger's factory, you cross the narrow land between the Mountains of the Clouds and the Sojar Sea."

The sky is clear, save where clouds cluster round the peaks. Closer are vast flocks—some of birds, some of little winged dinosaurs, and some of archaeopteryx and unknown species that mingle the traits of both. Above the flocks, scattered black dots drift against the blue of an atmosphere which appears as infinite as the New Mexico sky.

An follows my gaze. "The high specks could be Mahars or their pterodactyl servants or Krüger's flying machines," she says. "But they can't see what we are, either."

"None of them advance steadily, as a machine would." I turn to An. "Krüger's flying machines have eyes?"

"I don't know," she says. "I've never been near one. But when Krüger met with us, he had a machine-man with eyes. Maybe his flying machines have eyes, too." She gives me a grin. "My eyes see no man-eaters close enough to keep us in the trees."

Lowering its body, I send the lobster striding into grass the height of my waist. The species is unfamiliar, its stalks tipped by tiny flowers in delicate hues. Their fragile fragrance lures bees, whose hind legs are so thick with pollen they might be wearing pantaloons of solid gold. Where gaudier blossoms exhale, butterflies and hummingbirds make the air a treasury of living gems. There are bats, as well, ignoring the blaze of the sun as they dart among the blooms which lift from the magueyes on a rocky ridge.

My passenger startles me with a laugh. "Your machine-insect can go fast!"

I smile. "How did you come to learn English?"

"Abner started to teach the Mezops his language," she says, "but David decided only his closest allies—people like his mate and mate's brother and my cousin—should know English."

A private language would increase the Americans' power over the natives of Pellucidar.

"That, Ja didn't like," An continues. "So he secretly teaches me English as he learns more of it."

"Did Ja or Abner teach you measurements of distance, like miles or leagues?"

A line appears between her brows. "What difference does distance make, when one journey between two places might take one sleep, and another journey between the same places might take many sleeps?"

"I don't want to take several 'sleeps' to reach my mother, if we can rescue her in one."

An grows puzzled, then exclaims, "I keep forgetting. You're from far away, like David and Abner, who think we should all take our sleeping periods and waking periods together. That's ridiculous. A person should sleep or hunt when she needs to, for as long as she needs to."

"You don't care about day and ni—"

I close my mouth. How can the people inside the earth know about day and night, when their sun is always at noon?

"Abner and David say we need 'days' and 'nights,' 'hours' and 'minutes,'" An says, "but I don't see why. It's true you might leave your village for many sleeps, and return to find no one in the village has noticed you were gone, or go away for one sleep while they wonder if you were killed a dozen sleeps ago. But that's only natural."

My head is spinning. "How is that natural?"

"How could it be any other way?" An laughs. "Once I went fishing, and came home to find my younger sister had grown two finger-widths."

"Dear God," I say, with an involuntary glance at the clock on the instrument panel. "Time in Pellucidar is a wholly subjective phenomenon!" I look at An with pity, and a growing sense of horror. "You could return from helping me to find your family's grown old and died."

"'Grown old,'" she says. "That's what Abner did, in the place you come from. No one here does that. Death should come from war or the hunt. This 'growing old' must be a fearsome wasting disease."

As a blood-drinker who will never share Abner's experience, I can only say, "I suppose it is."

How mortals would seek entrances to the inner earth, if they realised the secret of eternal youth lay within.

Have many sleeps have passed for my mother since Maenck brought her to the earth's core? Is she already in Krüger's clutches? Has Maenck violated her? Does she still live?

Krüger wouldn't kill or assault her. He has no taste for matters of the flesh, and great ambitions for Germany and himself. He captured Clarimal and Winston Churchill last winter, intending to implant their brains with electrodes of his devising, which give him control of others' minds. If Krüger can control my mother, with her more than human abilities—

"Are you tired," says An, "or hungry?"

I've eaten since I drained the Steel Mask's blood, more than twelve hours ago. I examined the lobster before leaving the cavern on the surface and found tins of food and enameled bottles of water in the lorry-bed. I moved several of each to the back of the cabin before starting this journey.

"I'm all right," I tell An. "If you're hungry, I've food and water in the back seat—"

She looks over her shoulder, wrinkles her nose, and studies our surroundings.

The lobster is moving at the speed of an express train as it makes a half-circle around a herd of grazing triceratops. On a grassy ridge, a herd of fox-sized mammals watch us warily. They appear to be living examples of the "dawn horse," a species long extinct on Earth.

An rests her Rigby across her thighs and fires her Colt .45.

It would be an impressive feat were she standing on solid ground, but it's mostly vexation I feel as I halt our vehicle where the eohippus lies motionless, abandoned by its startled herd-mates.

I lower the lorry-body nearly to the ground and leave the engine quietly humming. There's no urgent need to turn off the vehicle when it won't need to refuel for decades. Besides, we might need to make a quick escape.

An returns her revolver to her holster, then picks up her rifle and steps onto the short-cropped grass.

While her back is to me, I leap onto the roof of the cabin, bearing the Mannlicher-Schönauer repeating carbine I found on first entering the cabin.

"Be quick," I tell An. "Maenck won't pause to hunt. And there's neither time nor fuel for cooking."

"Why would we start a fire?" She's eviscerating her kill with ease, though her knife has a knapped flint blade. "Smoke is visible a long way away."

"In this world, I suppose it would be."

She gives me an amused glance. "Are you like Abner, who always wants to burn meat?"

I find uncooked flesh far more appetising than cooked, but even a fur-clad savage must find that barbaric, so I make no reply.

"Raw is better," An says.

I hide my shock and begin turning in a circle to watch for threats.

As I take in the breadth and height of the range we've left behind, I forget to breathe. I've seen nothing like the Mountains of the Clouds save the world-wall of the Himalayas.

British intelligence sent me to India to investigate rumours of insurrection. M supposed my features would be taken for a half-caste's. And perhaps I would have found insurrectionists, if he'd included an East Indian language among the European and Mideastern tongues I was taught as a child.

Now I see a whole wild world the British Empire must claim and civilise before our enemies can.

It should be a joyful thought, but I find myself remembering tents and hospitals with their thousands of wounded, battlefields with their thousands of dead. Our enemies will never rest, and war requires resources. Britain cannot afford to let a rival empire seize the resources of an entire world—

Unbidden, a memory disrupts my thoughts.

India is the home of civilisations that were old when that mountain bandit Alexander doomed his ambitions in my father's land, a maharajah's daughter told me, last winter. *Do not think my ancestors were barbarians. And do not pretend Germany has less right to overthrow other nations than England.*

A tremendous crack returns my attention to my surroundings.

An gives a surprised laugh. "I didn't know there were lidi in this part of Pellucidar." Seeing my puzzled expression, she says, "Don't worry, that's just a lidi snapping its tail." Realising this explanation offers no enlightenment, she adds, "A lidi is a diplodocus. They use their tails to defend themselves from predators."

I consider what beasts might prey on a dinosaur eighty feet long. "I'm amazed humans aren't extinct in Pellucidar."

The breeze drops, but high grass stirs some fifty yards away. A creature resembling a wolf-dog rises into sight. It's the size of an Eriskay pony, and it's no sooner gained its feet than it's surging towards my travelling companion.

"Get in the machine-insect, An."

Though thunderous roars and bellows fill our ears, she looks towards the soft sounds of padded paws. Despite its massive build and heavy bones, the wolf-dog is gaining the speed of a leveret. An reacts by reaching for a nearby bush.

"Now!" I call, finger tensing on the trigger.

An steps into the cabin with her rifle, her field-dressed kill, and a broken branch bearing a few small fruits.

I swing into the driver's seat and get the lobster moving.

She looks at me with a frown. "Why didn't you kill the jalok?"

"I don't care to take another creature's life merely because you're careless of yours."

An rubs her hand where the fingers are missing. "When you have the chance, you should kill something now that might kill you later. On Luana, we've driven the large predators off the cliffs, so we don't need to worry about being attacked by land beasts."

I remember my mother finding my three-year-old self with a pile of dead badgers and hares and foxes.

You must hunt sometimes, to satisfy your blood-thirst. She lifted me so I rested against her hip, my arm on her shoulders. *Do you think it's right to take more than one animal at a time?*

I forgot I mustn't, I said, blushing with shame at how I'd abandoned myself to indiscriminate killing, like a vampire.

My mother smiled gently. *A butcher kills one beef-cow, not the herd, so he might always have meat later.*

I thought of milch-cows, and thereafter refrained from taking a deadly amount of blood from the animals I caught.

Was that the lesson she intended?

An's voice interrupts my thoughts.

"You're weak, like Abner," she says pityingly. "He says we shouldn't slay God's creatures wantonly. His people may worship a spirit which favours man-eaters, but we don't."

She points at the carnivore, where it has ceased its pursuit with a snarl of frustration.

"David says jaloks—hyaenodons—are long dead where he's from, so I suppose I need to warn you," she says. "A person with a spear or handgun doesn't have a chance against a jalok."

Then she laughs, and hands me a small cut of flesh from her kill, and feeds herself a bite.

"'In this world,' you said earlier," she says. "As if there is another."

"The world is like a bubble," I say. "My people and David and Abner's people live on the outside surface of the bubble. Your people live on the inside surface—"

An is laughing again. "You and David and Abner say this. The Mahars say the world is a hollow in infinite solid stone." She shakes her head. "The Mezops know the world is flat."

I look at the curve of sea and land rising before us, but don't argue. It wasn't so long ago that most people on the surface thought the earth was flat, though ships drop out of sight as they sail over the horizon.

An doesn't miss my glance. "The world has walls, of course. Otherwise, the water would all spill into the Molop Az, and foolish beasts and humans, as well."

She makes a gesture which takes in plain and peaks and sea.

"The world floats on the Molop Az—the Fire Sea," she tells me. "Have you never seen volcanoes? Have you never seen a buried body which was uncovered again, and noticed how parts have been borne away by the spirits which dwell in the fire? They're the reason my people and Ja's bury our enemies, and place our own dead in high trees. The birds bear our fallen ones piece by piece to the Dead World."

Many Christians say Hell occupies the centre of the earth, though most geologists say otherwise.

Most geologists also proclaim the earth solid.

"But these aren't things to worry about." With a smile, An passes me a fruit. "We have food!"

As we finish her kill, the air grows damp. Ahead, a lake rises with the curve of the plain. I alter our course to avoid the water.

An raises the last fruit by its stem. Like the rest, it's the size and hue of a pippin. Its shape reminds me of a Clyde Valley strawberry.

"Yours," An tells me.

"Thank you, but I couldn't."

"You're my guest in this land." She watches me with lazily lidded eyes. "Manners demand I give you the last bite."

I extend my open palm.

Her breathing and heartbeat and scent alter as she ignores my hand. "I'll feed it to you."

For Christ's sake. "I don't know you that well."

"You're controlling this fast machine, and I don't want to distract you," she says, as if we haven't been speeding at the same pace throughout our meal.

I alternate between taking bites of the fruit and watching our surroundings, and try not to think of the folk belief about feeding a heart-shaped strawberry to another.

I don't think An notices I've four teeth sharper and more prominent than those of mortals.

When she's tossed the core from the cabin, she places her left hand on the back of my right hand, where it grips the wheel. Her palm and surviving fingers are rough with calluses and scars. The contact sends a jolt through me like electricity.

She murmurs, "Do you want to rest?"

"If I get too tired to drive, I will sleep," I say.

"*Sleep?*" Her hand tightens on mine. "You feel like I do."

I hide my alarm. "Why do you say that?"

She smiles. "Your face is getting redder, and you're breathing faster."

If she's not lying, An doesn't have a nose or ears as keen as mine.

Still, she's too observant by half.

"Of course—" her smile widens "—you did seem quite interested in all of us in the tunnel."

"I was shocked to see naked people."

She pulls her hand from mine with an astonished look. "The Mezops are a wealthy and well dressed people."

"Where I'm from, wealth has nothing to do with it. You only see another person's face bare, and maybe his hands."

Her eyebrows pinch together.

"Why do your people cover yourselves like that?" she asks. "Don't you suffocate in the heat? Although—" her tone turns considering "—you don't seem to sweat."

It would be advantageous to know if her people know about blood-drinkers.

"Of course," she continues, "I could be wrong." Her heavy eyelids sink half shut. "I should remove those ridiculous layers to investigate."

Accurst savage. I don't want her. Yet I desire her.

To think I feared my mother would learn of my degeneracy from Clarimal.

"Nothing is going to happen between us, An," I say. "I'm rescuing my mother and taking her home."

She gives me a sleepy, suggestive smile. "I'll help."

"I'm grateful for your assistance," I say, "but you cannot go to our homeland."

An's smile vanishes. She studies my face, then speaks grimly. "Do you have a mate in your land?"

"A *mate*?" I say. "I don't have a mate."

"Well, then." An relaxes into her seductive smile. "I won't have to kill your mate and claim you as mine."

I burst into astonished laughter.

"That's not a custom of my land."

She leans towards me, exacerbating my attraction.

"If you don't have a mate, Luzia, why do you refuse me?"

"We barely know each other," I remind her.

Then I remember how few hours passed between meeting Clarimal and having her in my bed.

An says, "We—"

Egrets erupt around the lobster. It's run into ankle-deep water. I've misjudged the width of the swamp which rings the lake.

Water can't harm a British leg-lorry or tripod, but I've no idea what effect water might have on Krüger's lobster. And, while its striding-legs compensate for uneven ground as generously as a British leg-lorry's, that won't matter if a leg steps in a deep hole at our rate of speed. If the resulting tumble doesn't take our lives, the immense crocodiles in the lake may finish the task.

As I direct the lobster onto higher ground, An says, "You noticed I'm interested in you, at least. David and Abner seem blind to many things a child would notice."

"Many from our world don't notice," I admit, though I expect the operatives are merely ignoring native degeneracy. "Still, it's unwise for a woman to demonstrate desire for another woman in my world."

"Unwise?" An exclaims. "Why?"

"Because desire for members of your own sex is wrong."

"*Wrong?*" She laughs. "Why would anyone think *that?*"

"It's an inversion—" I notice her blank look. "It's a reversal of our natural desires."

"Nothing's reversed," she says. "The feelings are the same whether I desire a man or a woman."

I've never felt a difference between my desires for women and my desires for men. The similarity is like my disinclination to have a family. Both arise from my inhuman nature as a dhampir.

"You misinterpret your feelings," I tell An.

"I misunderstand my own feelings?" she says. "I've never heard a bigger load of lidi crap in my life."

"Whatever you feel, sexual inversion is wrong," I point out, "because it cannot result in children."

An bursts into laughter. "Next you'll tell me David should abandon his mate, because she hasn't borne children. Any adult who wants children can adopt them." Her humour fades as she watches a trio of enormous lionesses bringing down a small Megalosaurus. "Your land is fortunate indeed," she whispers, "if it has few orphans."

"You miss my point—"

An's laughter returns. "You don't have a point!"

"I should never have expected a Stone Age savage to understand," I say. "The wise men of civilisation—Ellis and Freud and Krafft-Ebing and many others—have scrutinised the sex drive with the impartial eye of science. They've proven the desire for one's own sex is a degeneration from ancestral health—a congenital defect to be conquered or suppressed."

An looks me up and down.

"I don't see any defects," she says. "And I know what science is. Abner and David use it to make muskets and cannons and steam-powered tools. Krüger uses it to make machines we don't have. Science has nothing to do with sex or desire."

I open my mouth to correct her, and close it again.

The geologists are wrong about the solidity of the earth.

The *Titanic* sank, a fate deemed impossible for the most advanced ship in existence.

The priests and philosophers proclaim vampires devoid of emotion and morality—and I nearly destroyed my lover before I realised they were wrong.

Why have scientists not learned the truths of vampire behaviour, I said to Clarimal, *when they've plumbed the truths of human behaviour?*

Have they? Clarimal said.

Is it possible the scientists are wrong about inversion?

"You're shaking," An says. After a moment, she touches my shoulder. "Have you taken ill?"

I can barely hear my own voice. "I was born ill."

An rests her hand on my shoulder and studies my profile so intently, it's all I can do not to turn away.

Finally, she murmurs, "Your wise men are fools."

Her surviving fingers tighten, her scent surrounding me as she leans close.

She fits her right hand to the far side of my face. The hand is intact but no less scarred or calloused than her left. Her flesh is warm.

Gently, she turns my head until our gazes meet directly.

Her lips brush mine—

Water splashes suddenly around the lobster-legs. A weight slams into An's side of the cabin with such force that the lobster nearly tips over.

I brake, but the abrupt stop fails to dislodge our attacker.

As An seizes her rifle, jaws like a crocodile's thrust through the window. I draw my revolver with inhuman speed, yet before I can fire between the parted jaws, they close, pulling An to the window. When her torso strikes the door, the fangs, sunk like daggers into her throat and chest, tear free. Scents of heated iron and salt fill the air as An's blood sprays me.

She slumps unconscious, her damaged heart faltering and torn windpipe whistling. I thrust my right hand between the jaws. My forefinger tightens.

Six rounds in the brain-pan, and the creature's heart continues its steady kettledrum beat.

Your little gun may kill a little dinosaur, but it'll do no good against large beasts.

The snout shoves more deeply into the cabin. Then it's gone, the carnivore falling. The impact shakes the earth.

I holster my Webley and curl my body over An's. I open my right wrist with my fangs and thrust my wound between her lips. As my blood flows into her mouth,

I use my free hand to pinch together the edges of her throat wound.

Through An's window I see our assailant. It's an amphibian the size of a Cape buffalo, with the form of a salamander, the legs of a toad, and the jaws of a crocodile. I recognise a labyrinthodon, extinct on the surface for over a hundred million years.

It leaps in the air and rolls on the ground, frenzied as the bronco at a Wild West show. Like a cowboy, the slight figure clinging to the labyrinthodon's back remains in place. The rider's head is lowered, mouth adhered to the side of the great beast's neck.

The thunder of its heartbeat cuts off and the labyrinthodon begins to collapse. The rider springs from its back. One gloved hand darts, seizing a motor-cycle rider's cap and goggles, which have snagged on a frond of bracken. The figure alights on the ground as gracefully as a cat and pulls on the cap with the goggles above the bill, then faces me directly, clad in the uniform of a despatch rider of the Royal Engineers Signal Services.

"I'll look for other threats," she tells me, removing the Mauser machine pistol from its holster on her belt, and leaps to the roof of the cabin.

"Don't think I'm not grateful for your assistance," I say over the sound of boots on metal. "But why the bloody *hell* did you ignore my wishes and M's order?"

Her voice comes to me. "Crocodiles the size of the leg-lorry are swimming towards us, and they're too numerous to share the dead amphibian. We should leave or utilise the heat-ray."

"I'm occupied. Care for a rifle?"

Clarimal Stein swings into the back seat and holsters her Mauser.

As I pass her An's rifle with my left hand, she speaks quietly. "The mortal's heartbeat is getting stronger."

"Her name is An." I match Clarimal's soft tone, knowing an unconscious mortal may hear and remember. "She's healing, but too damaged to cease taking my blood."

"If you'll move over, I'll drive."

"You've no experience with leg-lorries, and they've significant differences from other vehicles. I'll teach you how to pilot the lobster once you've told me why you're here."

Clarimal gives me a smile. "How could I let you go to the heart of the occupation with only a mortal at your side? The Austrians know who you are and how to destroy you."

"And the Austrians know who the Countess Karnstein is and how to destroy you." I shake my head in frustration. "How did you get here?"

"I drove my trusty Triumph to the Tann front." Clarimal slides the elephant gun through a window, tracking her prey. "On foot, I slipped through the Austrian lines. The crocodiles are quite fast, darling, even when they're not swimming."

"What happened next?"

"I made my way through the forest to the Tannschloss. Below the castle, the moonlight revealed a man resembling a young Sherlock Holmes, who was slipping from the secret entrance into the trees. I was down-wind and ducked out of sight, so your brother didn't detect my presence as he departed."

"Then you entered the hidden passages in the castle walls."

"And arrived in the cavern as you were investigating the leg-lorry," Clarimal says. "I kept watch from behind a stalagmite and, once you got in the lorry cabin, I hid myself in the back."

"Where the Cro-Magnons failed to observe you?"

"I leaped up to wrap my arms and legs around a cross-beam." She smiles. "Mortals rarely look up when doing searches," she says. "I'll need to shoot soon."

I brush a hand over An's wounds, and the dry blood crumbles and falls away to reveal smooth skin. Her respiration is untroubled, and her heart beats vigorously. Her scent confirms that my blood has restored her to full health.

Her scars and maimed hand show no change. My blood does little for old injuries.

Ignoring the exhaustion and throbbing headache of blood-loss, I keep a hand on An's shoulder to hold her upright as I bring the lobster to a run.

A glance finds Clarimal withdrawing the rifle from her window. "We've escaped the crocodiles, and no other carnivores portend." She sets her cap at a rakish angle that makes me smile despite my vexation. "Let me drive."

I face forward. "I'm fresh enough."

"After losing so much blood?" Clarimal says. "And you've not slept in two days—"

"Neither has Maenck, and I don't share his mortal weaknesses."

"Blood-drinkers aren't immune to fatigue, and your mother's kidnapper may reach his allies before we reach him." From the sound, Clarimal's opening a water bottle. "We should keep as fresh as possible," she continues. "I fell into *upiór* sleep after hiding in the back of the lorry, and—"

"You were in agony," I say, "because you had no coffin."

She meets my glare and holds out the open bottle. "I felt more pain in February, when I was last separated from my coffin."

We're crossing relatively level ground, so I take my hand from the steering wheel to accept the bottle. Draining the contents dulls my headache, but does little for my enervation.

When I've returned my hand to the wheel, I say, "I don't like you to suffer *any* pain."

"The pain ended with *upiór* sleep. But my waking—"

Clarimal falls silent.

Alarmed, I glance back. "Was it painful? That is new—"

"My waking was painless, as it's always been in my centuries of unlife," she says. "But it wasn't—*abrupt.*"

I don't disturb her in the coffin, but I witnessed this transition during our rescue of Churchill. In one second, there is only her expressionless aspect, her white face, the deadly stillness of her body, the coolness of her flesh, the lack of heartbeat and respiration for long minutes at a stretch. In the next second, her eyes are wide open, and there is the sharp indrawn breath, the explosive heartbeat, the hot tumult of her blood and the bright colour overspreading her countenance.

"What do you mean," I whisper, "'it wasn't abrupt'?"

"I woke—"

She falls silent. I look over my shoulder. She has the air of someone who has recovered something infinitely precious, thought lost forever.

"I woke slowly and luxuriously. I woke the way I used to, as a mortal."

I am suffused with amazement, like someone raised in darkness who stumbles into sunlight. "How can that be?"

"I can only suppose it's because this inside-out world has no sunrise or sunset."

"No sunrise or sunset." My pulse speeds like the lobster. "Might that mean you don't need your coffin in the Hollow Earth?"

"It might," she says quietly. "It might also mean I'll become as weak and fragile as a mortal."

I inhale sharply.

"There's no evidence that must happen," Clarimal reminds me. "But we know almost nothing about this world."

It's a capital mistake to theorise before you have all the data, my dear Lucy, my step-uncle told me, more times than I can remember. *Once you do, you begin inevitably to twist facts to suit your theory, instead of developing theories to suit the facts.*

"Whatever may befall," Clarimal continues, "I need to learn how to drive this vehicle."

I halt the lobster in a crouch beside a narrow brook and begin removing my driving gauntlets. "You have the wheel."

"And you need to eat," Clarimal replies. "I've opened some tins."

Her blood is as effective as mine in healing a mortal—but ancient lore says that if a vampire and a dhampir share blood, the dhampir will become a vampire.

Laying the gauntlets aside, I locate the spoon I took from the lorry-bed before I started this journey, and apply it to tins of Sauerkraut and Rinder Fleischkonserve. With An's rifle, Clarimal springs to the top of the cabin, to keep watch over our surroundings while we're immobilised.

Once my hunger is sated and my vigour restored, I step onto the bank of the brook and begin unbuttoning my shirt.

Where she's turning slowly about on the roof, Clarimal breathes, "This world." Her voice has the awe a soul must feel upon entering Heaven. "I've traveled the globe, and even witnessed Professor Challenger's unspoilt 'Lost World.' But in all my centuries, I've seen no place like this."

I think of our night under the North Atlantic stars and Clarimal's whisper as she faced me on the deck of the *Titanic*.

How fantastically unlikely that an Austrian girl should survive two centuries, to stand upon the deck of a foreign ship built with otherworldly technology, at the mid-point between continents, in the company of a British girl she should never have met.

I tense to leap onto the roof and sweep her into my arms, then remember the feel of An's lips on mine.

I remain where I am.

"It will infuriate M, should he learn of it," I say. "It must break my mother's heart, should she realise we're lovers. Yet I cannot help rejoicing that you're here with me."

Clarimal turns to me with a smile.

"You're removing your shirt." She raises her slim eyebrows. "We have time for intimacies?"

I return her smile. "We don't have time to fight every predator attracted by the scent of blood."

I remain alert for threats as I soak the bloody part of my shirt in the chilly brook. As I scrub the linen between my hands, blood flows free in bright streaks and curls.

The blood lures no piranha or tiger fish or dwarf caiman, but there's a fifteen-foot serpent swimming down the current, its wedge-shaped head lifted to watch me. Before it can strike, I grab the cottonmouth round the throat. As I toss it downstream, I remember An's warning.

When you have the chance, you should kill something now that might kill you later.

I wring out the damp portion of the cloth and tug out the wrinkles as best I might before I put on the shirt.

Then I wet a rag from the lorry-bed and go to the cabin. "An's still asleep," I say. "I'll move her to the back seat."

"You need to hold her," Clarimal tells me as she takes the driver's seat. "I'll need both hands on the wheel as I learn to pilot this machine, and a rough patch of ground might smash her head against the instrument panel. No amount of dhampir or vampire blood can repair harm to a mortal's mind."

I gather An in my arms. She doesn't stir. I slide onto the front bench, her head on my shoulder. My complexion heats.

"She sleeps deeply," Clarimal remarks.

With An in my lap, I fasten the seat belt about us. "She should sleep deeply, after a fang in the heart."

As I give Clarimal instructions, I use the wet rag to wipe the blood from the fur of An's tunic.

I've been a volunteer nurse and ambulance driver almost since the war started, nearly a year and a half ago. I've tended thousands of men and scores of women and a few androgynes in every state of injury and undress. Only now do I lose the ability to ignore the curve of a breast, the line of a muscle, the cinnamon of scent, the sight of bare skin, the heat and pressure of the body against mine.

I'm not even tempted to try my childhood acting lessons on Clarimal. My desire for An is as clear to her as lightning at midnight.

Once she's controlling the lobster, I ask a quiet question. "Did you overhear An's explanation of time in the Hollow Earth?"

Clarimal inclines her head. "It's as unpredictable as time is said to be in Fairyland."

She glances at me with a smile.

"I must say, darling," she says. "You and An have had some interesting conversations."

Clarimal and I have agreed not to refrain from intimacies with others when we're apart, and An is not even my lover, yet I flush nonetheless.

"Do I want to know everything you overheard?"

"You know I don't care to be an eavesdropper," she says. "But I woke as the mortals surrounded your lorry, and thought it best that no one realise I was present." Her smile returns. "I thought I'd learn what your seduction techniques are like when we're not together."

"Alas, you've learned only that I have difficulty resisting temptation, even when my mother's life is at stake."

Clarimal glances at the mortal. "Beauty and brains." She glances at me, and her smile widens. "No wonder you want her."

My complexion must be scarlet, but I summon a smile. "I was attracted to all the primitives in the passage. I merely respond to the presence of bare flesh."

Clarimal's expression sobers. "I became a predator when I was turned," she murmurs. "But you and An are born hunters. It's more than her flesh that attracts you."

"Sweet Hell, don't be daft. She's an ignorant savage."

"An ignorant savage?" Clarimal says. "I heard your discussion of the nature of sexuality. An's a natural philosopher."

"Whatever she might be, it won't include my bed-partner."

"I'm only saying, be careful," Clarimal says gently. "You might conceive a *tendre* for An."

"You must drink her dry before matters go any farther."

I speak lightly. But to fight for survival with some-one—to hold her against your heart as you save her life— these cannot leave you uncaring. If you also desire her…

Clarimal looks at the mortal again, and I realise her desire is stirring.

"An is alluring in every way." She gives me a puzzling smile. "She might fancy us both."

It takes me a moment to grasp her meaning.

Then it's as if she's plunged me into the Arctic Ocean, when I'd no idea we were within a thousand miles of water.

I can hardly speak. "Are you getting bored with me?"

"Tod und Teufel!" Clarimal says. "Du denkst Ich habe *das* gesagt?"

Clasping my hand, she holds it to her breast-bone as she presses her lips against mine in a lingering kiss which sets me afire—and her as well.

You cannot lie to a blood-drinker about desire.

When she draws her head back, she whispers, "Darling, I'm so sorry. I intended only a jest about the long, long existence of the blood-drinker."

"I understand," I murmur.

I keep forgetting. I've never expected to live as long as Clarimal has, though my father survived far longer. Blood-drinkers are usually destroyed when mortals discover our true nature, and the spread of literacy spreads knowledge of our existence. Too, the war shortens thousands of lives every day.

"I've never had two women at once," Clarimal says. "But we shouldn't pretend we might never want another woman to join us in our intimacies."

I capture my startled laugh between my teeth before I wake An. "Next you'll be telling me you want to sleep with a man."

She grins. "That has never happened since I was born in 1679. But I cannot say it never will." Her amusement fades. "We have stories about sexuality, and so do An's people, and—"

"She didn't tell me any stories about sexuality."

"She didn't need to. She doesn't understand our stories because her people have a story which lets individuals like us be happy with their desires."

I study Clarimal dubiously. "I wrote stories for the penny dreadfuls, before the war. Stories are a long way from the facts of biology."

"I refer to stories which explain or justify facts. Such stories aren't necessarily accurate, but once we believe one, we act to confirm it," she says. "We make stories, and stories make us."

"This is confusing."

"What is the story when intelligence operatives of the officially neutral United States make alliance with Dr Krüger?"

"Ah," I say. "The United States is secretly abandoning its neutrality to side with Germany and Austria-Hungary. Or the United States is neutral, but seeking to expand its empire by annexing territory inside the earth. Or the American operatives here are pursuing their own goal."

"An empire answerable only to themselves," Clarimal says, "in a world where the pinnacle of native organisation is the tribe, and the pinnacle of native technology the spear."

I take my hand from An's shoulder to rub my eyes. "Let's focus on rescuing my mother and let M worry about empires."

"Of course." Clarimal directs the lobster away from a herd of rhinoceroses larger than African elephants, then gives me a thoughtful look. "It would be helpful to know what story leads M to keep me away from your mother."

"We've already deduced his reason."

"Have we?" Clarimal frowns. "I've not read Stoker's book, for you've told me it includes a great quantity of nonsense—"

"I believe I said 'tommyrot.'" I hope the sudden tension in my gut doesn't reach my voice. "'Nonsense' is what I sold to the penny dreadfuls."

"—but I'd like to know what your mother told you."

I exhale. "I should have told you long ago, I know."

"Who wants to speak of horrors inflicted on her mother?" Clarimal rests her hand on mine. "I shouldn't have asked."

"Only because I should already have told you. An's asleep," I say. "It's as good a time as any to tell you what my mother told me."

Before I can speak another word, I'm caught in a cracking yawn.

"Sleep, darling," Clarimal murmurs. "I'll watch over An—"

I'm walking up Primrose Hill with my mother. She's taller than me, which hasn't been the case since I was ten years of age. No one else is about, this early in the morning.

The air is hot and close, but I'm eating freshly roasted chestnuts from a paper cone, and we're bundled in winter clothing. Snow covers the park, pure as a saint's soul. One of the Martian cylinders landed on Primrose Hill, but the Martians haven't invaded yet. They come to Britain in June of 1902, but it's Christmas Day in 1894 and I've just turned four years old.

"There," my mother says softly, in her middle-class London accent with its suggestion of an Irish lilt. "Do you see the waxwing?"

I follow her gaze to the Shakespeare Tree. "It's eating mistletoe berries."

"I know you'd prefer to hunt every day," my mother says, and I turn my head to find her watching me. "I enjoy hunting with my eyes. Do you think that's something you might like?"

Hunting for sights instead of blood is not something I've considered before. It seems poor sport indeed, compared to running alone through the night and bringing down a badger or fox with my hands and fangs. But I've only been granted the opportunity to hunt wild beasts four times a year, and I've not yet been sent to my third hunt at the Holmes family estate in Yorkshire.

I see my mother less often than I'd like. She must go away frequently, killing vampires and doing other secret work for queen and country. If I please my mother by hunting with my eyes, will she spend more time with me?

"I shall like looking for birds," I assure her, which I know is true, though it hasn't happened yet, because it will prove better than forgoing every sort of hunt for three months.

"Look!" my mother says. "It's Lucy."

We've had this conversation before—until this point. My mother didn't say these three words. Why would she, when I've been at her side all along?

I realise she's not looking at me, but at the young woman approaching us. I've never seen her before, but I recognise her. She's in the photograph of my mother with her dearest friend, for whom she named me.

"She's not gone," my mother tells me. "They told me it was necessary to destroy Lucy." She smiles at the woman joyfully. "They were wrong."

My mother hasn't told me this yet, but I know Lucy Westenra was turned into a vampire by Dracula, then destroyed by Miss Westenra's fiancé with the assistance of the vampire hunter Van Helsing.

I wake at a change in An's respiration.

She raises her head from my shoulder. Her eyes meet mine, and she smiles. She stretches in a manner which makes me only more aware of her weight, her exposed skin, her lithe beauty—

"Ah," she says, "I am refreshed."

I glance at the clock on the instrument panel. I've been asleep for an hour, or thirteen hours, or perhaps thirteen years. The damp section of my shirt has dried.

An runs her fingertips lightly over her throat and breast-bone, then touches a rip in her tunic below the collar-bone. She laughs. "Healed without a trace!"

I realise she doesn't know how gravely she was injured and assigns the disappearance of her wounds to the subjectivity of time in her world.

"You saved me from the sithic," she murmurs, slipping her arms round my neck, and tilts her face towards mine.

I draw my head back and turn my eyes to the side, and she twists about and sees Clarimal.

"I'm An the Mezop," she says. "Who are you?"

I say, "She's Clarimal Stein, a friend from the surface of the world."

"A friend?" An regards her coolly. "A friend followed you from as far away as you and David claim?"

Clarimal meets her stare levelly. "I'm Luzia's mate."

"My *mate*?" I stare at Clarimal, open-mouthed. "What are you talking about?"

Clarimal raises her left hand from her side, and I realise she's holding her machine pistol.

She points the Mauser at An's face. "If you think you can kill me and claim Luzia, you're in for some surprises."

An doesn't flinch, though the muzzle's bare inches from her brow.

She alternates a keen gaze between our faces and the firearm, then bursts into laughter.

"You have won, Clarimal Stein," she says. "Luzia remains your mate, and by wind and water, earth and fire, I vow not to woo her or fight you, for as long as you don't attack me."

"I've never wanted to fight you." Clarimal lowers her firearm. "You can take up your rifle."

An looks at me, and her expression turns as icy as the Matterhorn.

"You are unworthy of this magnificent woman, liar."

Before I can think of a response, she's claimed her Rigby and scrambled into the back seat.

Clarimal fastens her pistol in its holster and looks over her shoulder.

"Luzia intended no deception," she tells An. "She didn't understand your question, when you asked if she had a mate. In our world, the law allows only men and women to marry—that is the English term for mating under the law."

An scrutinises my face. Finally, she says, "You really didn't understand me." To my surprise, her expression turns sad. "What a strange place you come from."

I turn to my lover.

My mate?

In the back seat, An says, "We're about halfway to Krüger's factory now, Luzia."

The lobster's ascending a long, gradual slope threaded with brooks and scattered with bracken and boulders and rocky knolls and an increasing number of oak trees. Moss muffles the foot-falls of our lobster. Over the sounds of flowing water I hear the peep of frogs and buzz of insects and bellow of carnivores. Perhaps a thousand yards to our left, low waves plash on barnacled granite and make me wonder if tides exist in the Hollow Earth.

A cool breeze carries the cries of gulls and shags and the scents of seaweed and rotting fish and evaporating water. Shark fins little smaller than the mainsail of a dandy cut the open water. Beyond the fins, a head and undulant body interrupt the surface, betraying a creature I can only call a sea-serpent. Closer to shore, there are pterodactyls improbably swimming, and plesiosaurs who twist their snaky necks to watch our lorry run. The pterodactyls glance our way, now and again, but it's impossible to tell if this is idle curiosity or a more sinister interest.

The incline narrows as it rises to the gap between the terminus of the Mountains of the Cloud and the shore of the Sojar Sea. Perhaps a quarter of a mile ahead, the gap fills with oaks.

Clarimal says, "Does anyone else hear a droning sound?"

I realise I've been hearing the noise for a few moments.

An tilts her head, listening. "There's a faint buzzing sound, like Krüger's flying machines make."

Clarimal depresses the brake-pedal so quickly, we're thrown against the lap belts.

As Clarimal lowers the lobster-body to the moss, I observe a tiny shape in the western sky. It proceeds at a steady pace on a straight course. It resembles a bat but never moves its wings.

I draw the others' attention to the shape. "It fits the description of the automated monoplanes designed by Krüger."

Clarimal says, "It seems Krüger's bat-shaped aëro-planes weren't all destroyed by Agent G-8, as reported."

An says, "Krüger builds the flying machines at his factory near the Land of Awful Shadow."

"They're automated war-machines," I tell her, "armed with bombs and guns."

"If they use bombs and guns by themselves, his machine-bats do have eyes," An says.

"It's moving in our direction," I say. "If Krüger's monoplanes can recognise his lobsters, let's hope they cannot determine if one's been stolen."

"We're close to the wood," Clarimal says. "We'll keep still and hope to avoid notice."

An slides the barrels of her elephant gun through a window. "I'll keep an eye on the machine-bat."

While she's preoccupied, I quietly address Clarimal. "You weren't going to shoot An. Why the farce?"

"Her jest about killing a romantic rival indicates her culture accepts such activities," Clarimal softly replies. "She's no notion how to finish off a blood-drinker, but killing me would slow your mother's rescue. I needed to prevent an attempt on my life before she started."

"You also—you called me—" I clear my throat. "Do you think of me as your mate?"

"Before An said the word, I never thought of it," Clarimal says. "In my centuries of unlife I've had many lovers. I lived with none of them as I've lived with you." Her fingertip brushes my lips. "Who else can you be, Lucy?"

I hold her gaze as I raise her hand and kiss the palm.

At her window, An says, "The machine-bat continues in our direction."

I release Clarimal's hand to take up the Mannlicher-Schönauer, though I suspect bullets must have no more effect on Krüger's aëroplanes than they had on his mechanical men.

"While An's occupied," Clarimal says quietly, "I've another story I'd like to discuss."

"Sweet Hell," I mutter. "What story concerns you at a time like this?"

She surprises me with a smile. "The story which locates Hell in the centre of the earth, of course."

I'm startled into a laugh. "I must confess, I've also thought of Hell. But most modern men of God say Hell and Heaven exist outside the physical universe."

"Like Fairyland?" Clarimal's humour fades. "Whatever my failures of memory, I remember the miracle which turned water to wine. Yet many men of God condemn all alcohol as the express train to Hell. Why do some men of God invent stories and claim they come from God?"

"I suppose they believe those stories also come from God."

"That's the story many tell themselves," she says. "But some must deliberately create stories which let them manipulate people, because people fear they'll go to Hell if they don't do what the men of God say."

I stare at her.

A crease forms between her brows. "What is it, darling?"

"What if it's not just men of God doing that?"

"I don't understand," Clarimal says.

"Your soul was destroyed," I say. "Yet you have reason and emotion, talent and conscience. What purpose then does the soul serve, except to let God manipulate us?"

"*Lucy!*" Clarimal forgets herself so far that her voice rises. "How can you say that?"

"How can I not? It's a better explanation for the soul than any other I've heard."

"The machine-bat's getting closer," An says, raising her voice above the strengthening buzz of twin propellers. "So why are you two talking about souls?"

She leans an elbow on the seat-back between us. "Abner talks about souls and the Bible and God and religion," she says, "and wants us to have them. But these are ridiculous notions. You propitiate the spirits of wind and water and earth and fire so they will ignore you, and go about your business. You don't need anything else."

She returns her attention to the sky.

I look at Clarimal. "The loss of your soul, and your hope of Heaven for mine, once drove us apart," I say softly. "The pagan's correct in one regard. We're better off without souls."

This is a heresy sufficient to make my lover blanch despite her centuries as a vampire, but she answers quietly. "You both misunderstand my point. I mean that religion, like empire, is dangerous. Both have stories which can cause horrible damage—"

"I thought I saw something moving in the trees ahead," An says, changing the angle of her elephant gun.

As Clarimal and I turn to face the wind-screen, I say, "The earth has started trembling."

"Do you hear a noise—Tod und Teufel!" Clarimal says. "It's a stampede."

"A stampede," I say, "bound in our direction."

"If we move," Clarimal says, "the aëroplane may detect us."

"If it hasn't already," An says.

From the wood before us comes a boom so loud, it might betoken the collision of planetoids.

An frowns. "Why is a tyrannosaur so far from the plains?"

As I raise the Mannlicher-Schönauer, Clarimal depresses the heat-ray's switch to the warm-up setting and repeats an observation she made in Maple White Land. "I was a fool ever to want a look at Professor Challenger's pet pterodactyl."

As if on cue, a dozen dusky tyrannosaurs with crocodilian hides burst from the trees. When erect, the creatures must reach forty feet—more than twice the height of an African bull elephant. They're dreadful enough when they're bent almost double. Their footfalls send water and stones and shattered branches flying, and their weight shakes the earth as if to emulate the Avezzano quake. They boom and bellow, jaws gaping like cavern mouths lined with keen yellow stalactites and stalagmites.

Clarimal smiles grimly. "These dinosaurs are tools of Dr Krüger."

I've also noticed they have electrodes imbedded in their skulls, like the wolfmen who abducted Churchill.

Though the tyrannosaurs approach at a speed which elephants might envy, our heat-ray and bullets stretch eleven of the twelve dead on the ground.

The ray-severed skull of one dinosaur bounces against the lorry bonnet, crushing the brass heat-ray tube as our rifles exhaust their rounds.

Then the survivor is upon us.

I drop my carbine and fling open my door, to leap into the beast's reeking mouth. Bracing my boots on the floor, I catch the palate as the tyrannosaur recovers from its surprise and starts to close its jaws. I learn it's far stronger than I.

Spine bowing dangerously, I shout, "Your Mauser, Clarimal!"

Both women fire.

When I drag my battered body from the dead dinosaur's mouth, Clarimal's at my side, offering my carbine. "It's reloaded."

We confirm there are no further threats and examine the lobster. The severed tyrannosaur's head is resting on the lobster-claws, where it leans against the bonnet. The flaming neck is turned away from the lorry, but the weight of the five-foot skull should have crushed bonnet and claws. The damage is minimal.

"It appears Krüger's stolen the formula of the Martian aluminium alloy from Britain," I tell Clarimal softly.

An swings her freshly loaded rifle over her shoulder. Grinning enormously, she draws her knife. Then she begins sawing a trophy-claw from the nearest tyrannosaur forepaw.

"The monoplane's flying away with no alteration in course or speed," I say. "Let's hope it took no notice of us."

"We're going nowhere until we shift that skull," Clarimal says quietly to me. "We'll ask An's help, but the head must weigh almost a tonne, and she's no fool. If she realises we're not human, what shall we tell her?"

I smile. "A good story?"

Clarimal shakes her head, but her eyes light with amusement.

"We cannot risk firing the heat-ray device, with the tube damaged," she continues in a normal tone. "But if the head had crushed the engine, we'd be walking to Krüger's factory."

I've driven every sort of motor-ambulance and motor-car used by the Allies in Europe, and Clarimal has operated frequently in the guise of a motor-cycle despatch rider. We've learned how to repair every sort of petrol-, Diesel-, and spirit-burning vehicle. But we've no knowledge of how to repair the Martian-style engine I found when I took a look under the lorry bonnet, back in the cave.

This isn't to say I saw the engine. It's covered with lead, and I left it covered. I've no desire to pepper myself with burns and blisters, like the Curies and Einsteins and other scientists recruited to unlock the secrets of the Martian engine, or the labourers recruited to build our replicas.

As An helps us push the tyrannosaur skull off the lobster-claws, she studies Clarimal and me.

"Working together, David and Ja and I couldn't have moved so much weight," she says. "And you held a tyrannosaur's jaws open, Luzia, when it should have snapped you in half like a twig. Why are you two so strong?"

Clarimal looks at me, head angled so An doesn't see the inquisitive lift of her eyebrows.

"Your world has different kinds of spirits," I tell An. "So does ours."

"We need our spirits to ignore us," An says. "How do you persuade yours to make you so strong?"

"Clarimal and I are blood spirits," I say, "made flesh—"

Bullets shatter my shoulder and ribs before I hear the crack of elephant guns.

As I stumble, several things happen.

An collapses, blood flowing from her right temple.

Clarimal sinks down with a hole above her heart.

A pair of rifle-toting young men with Teutonic features and European mufti emerge from the wood. Each wears the crown of electrodes which Krüger designed for controlling the creatures he's implanted with his electrodes. Accompanying the mortals are a dozen mechanical men, aiming Rigby rifles for a second round of shots.

I think, *The tyrannosaur stampede was only a distraction—*

The metal riflemen fire.

"Krüger wants you dead."

It's a familiar voice which wakes me to pain and thirst, but I keep my eyes closed.

I'm lying spread-eagle on my back. Heavy iron cuffs weight my wrists and ankles. The air holds the hint of a chill. The odour of garlic obliterates any other smell.

There are birds nearby, singing unfamiliar songs. More distantly, dinosaurs shriek and bellow. Heavy rhythms of metal against stone worsen the throbbing of my skull.

Where I am in the vastness of the Hollow Earth, I've no idea.

Slitting my eyes open does little to dispel the mystery, because I'm lying in a canvas-roofed lorry-bed.

At my side, Lt Adalbert Maenck crouches, looking at me. He's about my size, and he still wears mufti which resembles my mountain-man disguise. Though he's as fair as I'm dark, a stranger might suppose he's come to free a fellow countryman.

We're alone.

"You've vexed Krüger too greatly to be considered for electrode implantation, it seems," Maenck continues, still speaking English. "You've vexed me, as well, Miss Harker. You chased me like a Westphalian brach, until I hadn't time to do more than grab your mother's bubbies."

I react by not so much as a twitch of an eyelash.

"So Krüger won't mind if I have a bit of it first, will he?" Maenck says. "And you're asking for it, naked like that."

As I'm fully clothed, "naked" must refer to the holes which have multiplied in my shirt.

The Luthanian gestures at a wooden stake, short-handled hammer, and braid of garlic which rest beside him on the floorboards.

"Not quite the sceptre of Lutha, are they? But the kingship is mine, once I've destroyed you and returned to the surface."

Careful to make no noise, I try my limbs against the taut chains holding me captive. I'm not as weak as I'd be if I'd returned from the dead. Still, I'm too drained to break my shackles.

Maenck picks up the braid of garlic and tickles my throat with the roots of the lowest bulb. The stink fills my nose and throat like a poisonous liquid. I keep my eyes nearly shut.

"Krüger doesn't want me taking women," Maenck says, "but you're not a woman, are you?" He smiles. "I'll have my way with you before I finish you off, monster."

I cannot decide if he thinks me aware or unconscious.

He removes his Tyrolean hat and lays it on the boards behind him. Turning back to me, he drops the braid. It strikes my windpipe with the heft of a hawser, and I cannot restrain a cough.

"Don't worry," Maenck tells me with a laugh. "I'll be as gentle as a monster."

His back-hand blow splits my cheek. His other hand seizes a handful of my locks, pinning my head to the floor as he lowers his lips towards mine. Hair rips from my scalp as I strike like a serpent, fastening my fangs in his neck. He opens his mouth but makes barely a sound, with my lower cuspids sunk in his trachea.

He reaches for his Luger. My hand closes on the lower end of his holster. Discovering I've strength enough to hold his sidearm fast, he reaches for his sabre, sheathed beyond my restricted range.

Many a cavalryman never sharpens his sabre, using it as a sort of bludgeon, lest the blade become stuck in a body. Maenck is a true sabreur. His edge opens my gut to the spine before he slumps unconscious.

When I've emptied his body of blood, I jerk my limbs. Iron links snap like snail-shells. Pieces fly across the lorry-bed, striking wood and canvas. A link rings on the metal support beam to which one chain is fastened. The bloody sabre and bullets forced from my flesh thump to the planks.

I wait, listening.

The nearest birds have fallen silent, but the other sounds outside the lorry-bed continue undisturbed.

I spring to my feet with the ease of a mongoose. All pain is gone, and energy crackles through me like electricity. Dried blood flakes from my injuries, revealing unblemished flesh. Breaking my cuffs as if they were crusts of ice, I lower them to the planks.

Quietly, I address the dead man.

"Perhaps Krüger said nothing about touching me because he thought you weren't stupid enough to try it before killing me."

As I'm disarmed, I appropriate his gun-belt and weapons.

"You might also have confirmed whether garlic affects me," I tell him. "It's got no power over blood-drinkers, unless you've a quantity sufficient to deaden our sense of smell."

I peek past the curtain hanging at the back of the bed, to find two other lobster-lorries. All are parked in the shade of chestnut trees so laden with burrs, they start me wondering about seasons in a world of eternal noon. Behind the lorries, a brook wanders among mossy stones, finally disappearing through a grate in a high stone wall with a lowered portcullis. Beyond the wall, a plain curves gently upwards, swarming with prehistoric beasts.

I'm unsurprised to see a mechanical man with a Rigby rifle pacing the battlement.

As the mechanical's not facing me, I drop the garlic over the tail-gate.

By making a discreet sabre-slit in the canvas wall on either side, then crouching to peer through the narrow horizontal opening in the back wall of the lorry-cabin, I'm able to reconnoitre the rest of my surroundings.

The small chestnut grove is contained within a fortress of four high stone walls, each patrolled by a Rigby-bearing mechanical. Where each pair of walls meet is a turret, surmounted by a full-sized heat-ray device manned by a mechanical. Just outside the grove is a small stone house, whose roof bears a singularly complicated Marconi aërial. The house is in deep shadow, as are the wall and plain beyond the house. Does a storm portend?

On another side, a factory rears beyond the trees, its windows sun-bright in a wall of fitted stone.

I mutter, "How'd Krüger get a factory built in only ten mon—ah. Why do I keep forgetting? Time means nothing in the Hollow Earth."

Beyond the factory and the fortress wall, a long ridge snakes to a solitary mountain that might dwarf Aconcagua.

"The Great Peak, I presume?"

About two-thirds of the way up the slope is a structure which must be enormous. Its towers are sharp as black blades against the snow. Round the towers and peak, tiny figures fly.

Krüger has his own alliance with the human tribe of the mountain near his factory, and a city of feathered Mahars.

If there are Mahars or pterodactyls nearby, I cannot tell, with canvas and leaves hiding most of the sky.

The immediate threat is the metal riflemen. I've no notion where to aim bullets to destroy them, assuming they even have a vital centre. A heat-ray would reduce the mechanicals to slag, if I could reach a working device before they noticed me. But melted automata cannot long go unnoticed, even in a world without time.

Escaping the lorry-bed is challenge enough. If I cut a larger hole through the canvas on either side, I might step through the wall, but must attract the mechanical men's notice. As for the opening in the back wall of the cabin, it's a narrow slit to allow back bench passengers to fire on foes behind the lorry. My inhuman strength might eventually tear the Martian alloy until the opening were large enough to slip through, if the metal made no horrid shrieks that would attract the mechanicals.

My pulse quickens as I discard my shirt, don Maenck's shirt and hat, and lower the tail-gate. Then, leaving his weapons on the belt, I step to the ground under the camera-lens eyes of the mechanical on the facing battlement.

The mechanical turns away.

I exhale in relief. It's one thing to suspect Krüger's mechanicals might mistake me for Maenck if I dress and act like him. It's another to test the hypothesis.

I find no one in the cabin of my lorry or in either of the other vehicles. In my cabin, Clarimal's cap and goggles lie abandoned. The engines of all three vehicles are shut off, but there are keys in the ignition switches. The only weapons are the heat-ray devices affixed to the front benches. The damaged device remains unrepaired, but I remove the switch-relay from all three devices and put the switches in one of my pockets.

As I approach the house, the sky becomes visible beyond the grove. I see no Mahars or pterodactyls. Yet I freeze, as if struck by some Arctic analogue of the Martian heat-ray.

The house isn't shaded by a cloud.

Krüger's factory is beyond the Sojar Sea, beside the Great Peak. It's not one of the Mountains of the Cloud, but stands near the Land of Awful Shadow.

The Awful Shadow is cast by a small planet barely a mile overhead.

I find the Luger in my hand, aimed as if to prevent the planetoid from crushing me.

I realise the little world must orbit the sun at the same speed as Earth revolves, if it always darkens the same portion of the inner surface. I cannot estimate its size accurately, when I don't know the diameter of the sun which swells behind it, but I doubt the planetoid is larger than Ceres. However, that remote rock may not possess mountains and oceans, plains and forests.

The birds bear our fallen ones piece by piece to the Dead World.

If this satellite is the Dead World of Mezop mythology, it may be misnamed.

The side facing me is dark. I discern no lights or other evidence of habitation. Still, humans seem no more unlikely on the planetoid than on Earth's interior surface.

Mountains slip out of sight along one edge of the satellite and into sight along the other. Realising the sphere is revolving on its axis, I suppress a laugh. The world within this timeless world has days and nights.

It's foolish to think the planetoid may fall from the sky, but it requires no little force of will to lower my firearm and walk into the shadow.

The closest window of the house reveals an unoccupied kitchen. Its electric lights are dark and its ceiling fans motionless, though there are wind turbines generating electricity on the ridge. Remembering how Krüger arranged my electrocution on the *Titanic*, I brush a fingertip across the metal door-knob. Receiving no shock, I try the knob.

The door opens with barely a sound.

I realise my nose has recovered when I'm assailed by stale smells of coffee and fried onions and meat. The smells don't obliterate the traces of rose and thymol and garlic. I follow these commingled odours to a pair of blank metal doors.

I look through the narrow gap between the doors. Though I crane my neck, I cannot see the entirety of the brightly lit space within. I see enough.

Pushing through the doors, I step into an operating room.

I aim Maenck's semi-automatic. "Drop the scalpel."

"Herzlich Willkommen, Fräulein Harker!" Krüger replies merrily, his smile revealing teeth like tombstones.

He faces me with a mechanical surgical assistant on either side. His great bald head wobbles on his scrawny neck, and his washed-out eyes seem tiny behind the thick round lenses of his spectacles. His appearance may be ridiculous, but his mind is England's greatest threat.

He wears a white surgeon's gown and India rubber gloves. One hand holds a scalpel above the white-draped figure on the surgical table before him. The hidden figure has a dreadfully slowed heartbeat. The smells of disinfectant and garlic and roses aren't quite enough to obliterate the figure's scent. My stomach tightens.

Two sets of sturdy heartbeats come from within the canvas tarpaulin shrouding a large, boxy shape behind Krüger.

"I expected you'd finish that impetuous fool of a Luthanian." Krüger is speaking English now. "Why didn't I hear you fighting my machine-men?"

"Aging ears?"

"No matter," he responds with a laugh. "I've learned to plan for your devilish ingenuity."

His gesture takes in the walls on either side, which I couldn't see from the doors.

Along the walls are twenty mechanical men, ten to a side. They're armed with a miscellany of rifles and portable machine-guns and heat-ray devices. Every muzzle targets my heart.

I face Krüger. "You received word of my approach from a pterodactyl or Mahar or automated monoplane."

"My allies' pterodactyls keep an eye on the Americans' little empire," he says. "My monoplanes oversee my territory, as you may verify for yourself."

He points with his scalpel.

Turning, I discover a pair of sturdy wall-shelves, one on either side of the doorway. Each shelf holds several bakelite boxes. Each good-sized box has a glass lens perhaps five inches across in the centre of its face. Each lens holds a different aerial photograph.

Krüger laughs. "I trust you enjoy these views from the skies of the Pellucidar."

I shiver as I realise every photograph is a moving picture.

"Every one of my monoplanes is equipped with a visual wireless transmitting device of my invention," he continues. "I call it telephotography."

As I turn back to Krüger, he speaks again.

"I was so delighted to learn of your arrival, I sent two of my nephews—several are helping me here—to greet you, along with some of my pet tyrannosaurs." His smile widens. "I'll have an impressive squad of monsters indeed, once I've implanted my electrodes in your corpse, your mother, and one other."

He pulls the tarpaulin from the boxy shape behind him, revealing a sizeable cage with three occupants. He gestures grandly at the figure on the surgical table within the bars. The figure lies motionless, facing upwards, like a body on a bier.

"It's convenient the Countess Karnstein is dead," Krüger says. "But if she resurrects before I've performed her surgery, she won't escape."

The thick iron bars of the cage are cruciform. Every bar is twined with wild roses and hung with braided garlic. Sacred wafers crowd the key-hole of the barred door.

Clarimal isn't alone in the cage. An the Mezop and the missing Prince Peter of Blentz are seated on its cross-stamped iron floor. They face Clarimal's table, their backs to us. An's head is tilted back, resting on the bar to which she's shackled. Blentz is similarly confined, but his head and torso slump forward. Both mortals are as still as Clarimal.

A chain loops Clarimal's body and legs, to bind her to the tabletop. Many of the heavy links are hung with crucifixes. A massive padlock fastens the chain, a sacred wafer in its key-hole.

Krüger turns back to me with a smile. "The prince and the primitive will be fine fodder for you and your paramour, once you've both resurrected in my control.

But our chatter grows tiresome." He gestures at the armed mechanicals. "Maschinenmenschen, absch—"

His command to fire breaks off as Clarimal snaps her chain and springs from the table. Pupils glowing red, she wrenches a pair of bars apart. Before Krüger can finish reacting to the noise, she's disarmed and captured him.

"You were surrounded by holy objects!" he screams. "How can this be?"

"How can it *not* be?" Clarimal shows her fangs in a smile. "There aren't ten mortals in the Hollow Earth who believe in God."

We make stories, and stories make us.

"Now, Krüger," she continues, "it would be wise to instruct your machine-men to put down their weapons."

As he complies, I draw back the sheet of his surgical table. I've a good idea what to expect. Still, the sight strikes me like a stake.

Stirring groggily, the woman on the table opens clouded eyes, which drift to me with no sign of recognition.

More than a dozen empty bottles of morphia lie with the surgical tools on a little steel table. It's impossible to drug or intoxicate a blood-drinker. It's merely difficult to drug or intoxicate my half-brothers or mother.

I raise my mother gently, until her head rests against my shoulder. I bite open my left wrist and press the bleeding wound to her lips. When I was a small child, she would raise me to her shoulder, offering her wrist because I couldn't hunt. The recollection twists the metaphorical stake in my breast.

I start as An's cuffs fall off, crashing to the floor and spilling broken bolts. In the cage, she springs lithely to her feet. As she turns, I see the shallow wound has disappeared from her temple. Her eyes are alert, her mind unharmed. A trace of blood streaks the side of her mouth.

As she sees what I'm doing, she grins. "You and Clarimal *are* blood spirits."

"Chains don't bind tightly," Clarimal is telling Krüger. "When you stepped out of the room, I slipped out of mine and drained Blentz, then slipped back into the chain to feign death."

But before you returned to the table, I think, you broke An's bonds and healed her with your blood.

"If you're as smart as they say, Krüger," Clarimal continues, "you'll order your machine-men to leave."

Krüger's expression twists, but when he barks an order, it sends every guard and surgical assistant out of the surgery.

The red light is fading from her eyes, but her fangs remain extended as Clarimal smiles at me. "Darling, you must be simply famished."

"Say your prayers, Krüger." I show my fangs. "I've waited years to taste your blood. And England's survival requires your death."

"Miss Harker, you will step away from Dr Krüger."

As he speaks, M pushes through the double doors, moving with an ease denied him in wintry Europe. My half-brother enters, halting beside M. Quincey aims his portable machine-gun at Krüger's heart as lightly as a normal mortal aims a Ruby pistol.

I say, "How the devil did you two get here so fast—right. We're inside the earth, where time means nothing. How the devil did you get here at all?"

My brother reluctantly turns his gaze from our mother. "Used my tripod to break through the Austrian lines," he tells me, "then used its tentacles to bash an opening into the cave."

M says, "I followed Quincey's fighting-machine here with three British leg-lorries and threescore British infantrymen. We've melted Krüger's automata and captured his fortress."

"How'd you find us?"

M's eyes examine my mother narrowly as he answers me.

"On arriving in the Hollow Earth, we captured and questioned a pair of American agents and their cavemen, and reached an agreement. Then it was a matter of following the Americans' directions—"

He falls silent as my mother shoves my arm aside and sits upright, staring at Clarimal with a look of dawning horror.

Her lips form silent words. "That's a vampire."

She reaches for Maenck's stake at my gun-belt with inhuman speed, but I'm faster.

"It's all right, Mother," I murmur, pinning her arms with an embrace. "The vampire won't hurt you."

She stares at me as if I've proposed giving her husband to a German torture squad.

Then she surges against my arms with a ferocity which nearly liberates her, despite my superior strength.

"We've got to kill it," she says, voice rising. "That's the vampiress Carmilla!"

At the doorway, M starts. Quincey turns so pale his freckles show like spots of blood on his countenance. He shifts his machine-gun to target Clarimal and turns his eyes to me.

"The Countess Karnstein would no more hurt you than I would," I assure our mother as I give my half-brother a slight head-shake. "She's an operative in the service of the British Empire."

M says, "Miss Harker, be silent!"

"That's not possible," my mother tells me, voice wavering as if she's found a dear friend dead. "It's a vampire."

She's the one who taught me to hunt the undead. As a dhampir, I'm born to protect humans from vampires. But without her, I'd not have survived to adulthood.

"Countess Karnstein is as loyal to England as you or I," I tell her gently. "I've mentioned it before, that vampires have emotion and share our ability to choose between good and evil."

My mother looks at me incredulously. "They do?"

M seems to shrivel, as if eviscerated by a ghostly hand. "I told you to keep Karnstein out of this, Harker."

I answer my mother reassuringly. "They do."

She whispers, "They told me Lucy would never retain her wits or emotions, or the ability to refrain from evil, once Dracula turned her."

I start at my name, then realise she's not talking about me.

"Because she lost her soul, they told me, Lucy could never be anything other than a mindless, murderous monster."

The blood drains from my head, and I grow dizzy.

Wilhelmina Murray Harker Holmes is the strongest person I know. She ignored the scorn of the world for a divorced woman. She raised the child of the vampire who forced her. She slays vampires single-handedly and faces the world as if it has no power to harm.

She sags against me, her eyes filling with tears.

"They destroyed my closest friend, and they didn't need to."

What have I done?

I look at M. My lips move, but I find no breath for sound as I say, "Why didn't you tell me?"

He reads my lips. "How could you not know," he shouts, "when you have my training and my brother's, and bear Miss Westenra's Christian name?"

The red glow rekindles in Clarimal's eyes. "Why did you assume your step-daughter would think that, Mr Holmes, when she learned the truth about vampires years ago?"

Why did I think my attraction to women was the problem?

"Oh, God, Mother," I whisper. "Can you ever forgive me?"

Ignoring the evidence of Clarimal's wrath, M advances on us. "You blood-drinkers will keep away from my wife."

The husband's claim is greater than the child's. I release my mother to M's arms and step to Clarimal's side.

M draws my mother close, murmuring, "If I'd known you then—if I'd known what was happening—it wouldn't have happened."

I look at Clarimal's prisoner with all the fury I cannot unleash on M.

"I grow thirsty."

Krüger sees my expression. For the first of all the times I've faced him, he flinches.

"Miss Harker." M's voice is sharp as a scalpel. "Stay away from Krüger."

I turn to M in surprise. "Leaving our most dangerous foe alive to escape is a risk we cannot tolerate."

"You've done quite enough damage for one mission, Miss Harker. Now, I said, 'stay away.' I need to talk to Krüger."

The red glow fades from Clarimal's eyes, which must betoken no less an act of will than my self-restraint.

M looks at my brother. "Take your mother out of here."

When Quincey has escorted our mother from the operating room, M points his Webley at Krüger's brow.

"It's the end of the line, Dr Krüger," M says. "Your string of unmatched inventions is done, your access to inner-earth resources lost, your brilliant mind destroyed. Unless you swear loyalty to England."

I blink at my stepfather. "What—"

"Well, Herr Doktor?" says M, keeping his attention on Krüger. "It would be a pity to destroy a mind like yours. But, while time in the Hollow Earth may be timeless, I'm not prepared to wait forever for your response."

"I love Germany as I've never loved anyone," Krüger says. "But the world cannot afford the loss of my mind, which has no match in history. Of course I agree to your terms."

"What the bloody Hell?" I say. "M, you can't—"

"Is Prince Peter of Blentz dead?" M says.

"I killed him," Clarimal says.

Simultaneously, An says, "That man?" She turns away, indicating Blentz. "Clarimal drank his—"

M shoots An in the head.

A moment—an eternity—I don't know how much time passes.

Eventually, I find my voice. "What have you done?"

"Maintained the secrecy of my mission," M answers.

I go to An. Kneeling, I feel her wrist for a pulse, though I know the bullet instantly stopped heart and breath. My blood heals the most dreadful damage to a mortal in life. It's no use to a mortal in death.

I look at M.

"Why?"

I cannot make a sound, but M's hearing has failed too greatly for him to realise it.

"We can't have any outsider knowing we've gained a valuable asset like Krüger," he replies.

"Who would she have *told*?"

He says, "We've ensured she tells no one."

I realise I'm shaking.

"She was our ally," I say. "I'd never have found your wife without her help. I shall inform Churchill—"

"I'm acting on his orders."

Defending the Empire justifies everything.

I smooth my palms down my arms and firm my shoulders to suppress my shivers.

"Is King Bernhard another valuable asset?"

"Unfortunately," M replies, "the blood you provided him failed to arrest his deterioration and death."

A sufficient draught of my blood never fails a mortal.

I stand, facing the head of British intelligence.

"Lutha must be in mourning, for he defended his mother's homeland valiantly," I say. "Still, Lutha will be better off as a protectorate of Britain."

"Miss Harker, I'm relieved you've finally perceived the obvious," M replies impatiently, and turns back to Krüger.

In Clarimal's expression I see sorrow, but no surprise.

Black as the Pit from pole to pole.

But the sun at the earth's core shines down infernally, and Clarimal watches from the base of the tree, where I've asked her to remain.

There's no one else in the grove.

In the largest of the chestnuts, An lies on her back where three great boughs meet. I lay her hands on her breast, where the bandoliers cross, and adjust her rifle beneath her hands. A gust stirs suddenly, rustling the leaves, and is as quickly gone. I brush the disordered locks of hair from her face.

From where I stand, you might almost think she's asleep.

I kiss her lips.

Though I jump from a great height, the impact fails to break a bone.

As I stagger, Clarimal reaches to catch me, and I shake my head.

"Get in the lorry."

After a moment, she fulfills my request.

My mother and Krüger, his identity concealed by a hood, are gone with M and a score of soldiers in one of the British leg-lorries. They've left twoscore infantrymen behind. Most of the remaining men guard the factory, where my brother and M's chosen commanding officer are meeting with Krüger's factory-foremen nephews, a cave-man chief, and a feathered Mahar, to forge a treaty with the local human tribe and the local Mahar city.

Clarimal has seated herself behind the steering wheel of the lobster-lorry we've stocked for our return to the outside world. I seat myself on the far side of the heat-ray device, not looking in Clarimal's direction, though I know she watches me.

She turns the key and starts the engine.

I speak. "You knew."

"I never imagined M would kill An," Clarimal says softly. "I knew only that sooner or later, in the service of your empire, you would see your empire commit an atrocity."

Finally, I look at her. "How did you know?"

"The story of empire is like the story of religion. It sanctions everything."

"Now I know how you feel," I say, "having the deaths of innocents on your conscience."

"I would point out you didn't kill An," Clarimal says, "but I know you'll never believe it."

"I told her she didn't have to go with me, when I should have thrown her out of the lorry."

"She knew the risks—"

"Not that one!"

I drive my fists at the glass, needing my flesh slashed to ribbons.

Clarimal catches my wrists.

Always, she's too fast for me.

"It doesn't help to hurt yourself. I know." When she feels the resistance go out of my arms, she releases them. "Anyway, the wind-screen wouldn't have served your purpose. The panes must be safety glass."

"Christ in Hell," I whisper. "Whom have I *not* harmed?"

"Lucy—"

"Why did I never realise how my mother must feel, if she saw a vampire who's become what her dearest friend was never allowed to be?"

Clarimal lays her hand on mine. "You had no reason to."

I turn suddenly to her. "You tried to warn me!"

Her hand tightens.

"I should have asked what befell her long ago," she says. "We both erred."

I make no response.

After a while, she raises her free hand to the steering wheel and starts the lobster moving slowly towards the fortress wall. The British infantrymen on guard duty don't challenge us as our lobster approaches the opening.

The portcullis is gone. My brother tore it out with the tentacles of his fighting-machine to admit M's party. Now the tripod stands, unoccupied, just outside the fortress wall.

I take my last look at An's body.

I think of a chained man's murder.

Clarimal's fingers lace through mine. "We've maps now."

I understand her point. "We'll visit An's island and tell her family."

The lobster's racing across the plain towards Mountains of the Clouds when I speak again.

"These aren't the first or the last atrocities from the British Empire."

There's a shudder in Clarimal's sigh.

"As long as Britain believes the story of empire," she says, "British atrocities are inevitable."

"I love my country," I say. "My empire—"

I turn to Clarimal.

"At the start of the war," I say, "I proposed that we enter the British Secret Intelligence Service to help my homeland end the conflict begun by Germany."

She looks at me.

"I agreed to serve the British Empire for as long as you do."

"We'll stay in the Secret Intelligence Service," I tell Clarimal. "But we shall serve Britain no longer."

Holding my gaze, my mate raises my hand and brushes the back with her lips.

She says, "We'll fight the British Empire until it's destroyed, or we are."

About the Author

Cynthia Ward has published stories in *Analog*, *Asimov's*, *Black Cat Mystery*, *Nightmare*, *Weird Tales*, and other magazines and anthologies. She edited *Lost Trails: Forgotten Tales of the Weird West* Volumes 1-2 (WolfSinger Publications) and has a pair of anthologies forthcoming in collaboration with Charles G. Waugh (Sam Teddy Publishing). With Nisi Shawl, Cynthia coauthored the fiction-writing handbook *Writing the Other: A Practical Approach* (Aqueduct Press). The first book of her Bloody-Thirsty Agent series, *The Adventure of the Incognita Countess* (Aqueduct), was a finalist for the Gaylactic Spectrum Award for Best Novel.

Made in the USA
Las Vegas, NV
22 October 2021

32895367R00066